PAINTSLINGER

Paintslinger is first published in Great Britain in 2020 by
Dark Cosmos Creative, Ltd, Cell Block Studios,
Portsmouth, PO1 3LJ

www.darkcosmoscreative.com

www.paintslinger.world

This is a work of fiction. Names, characters, places and incidents are either the product of the author's imagination or are used fictitiously, and any resemblance to actual persons, living or dead, business establishments, events, or locales is entirely coincidental. The author does not have any control over and does not assume any responsibility for third-party websites or their content.

Text copyright Jeremy K. Hardin, 2020

Cover and chapter illustrations
copyright Elizabeth Boyle, 2020

Editing by David Ekrut

Layout and design by Jennifer Ekrut

The moral right of the author and illustrator
has been asserted in accordance with the Copyright,
Designs, and Patents Act 1988

ISBN: 979-8568359579

PAINTSLINGER

JEREMY K. HARDIN

CHAPTER ONE

The universe, while somewhat inaccurately named, played host to many types of life, death, and rebirth throughout its many galactic clusters.

In an old galaxy, near the black hole heart, a system of dyson spheres thrived and like the universes it connected to, played host. A bar orbiting a binary black hole, complete with pulsar jet served some of the best nanodrinks in this junction of universes, this celestial crossroads.

An artist settled in the back of the zero gravity bar. She had her goggles off, her bandanna around her neck, and her easel and mixing tent all packed up at her feet. If anyone tried to relieve her of said items, she had a couple brushes and premixed cartridges ready to go in a bandolier across her front. For now though, she wasn't righting any wrongs.

In other times and realities, crossroads were places of danger, and this bar at the junction of universes was no different. A place of brief rest, a place of nourishment, and if anonymity came along for the journey, all the better.

This particular establishment, *PAN'S SHADOW*, served the best nanodrinks in the neighbouring universes, and being zero gravity allowed the space-bourne—those as had never tasted the weight of their mass—to visit without ill or harm. A kindness.

Mayhap the only kindness of this place. In zero g, the stations, tables, hovels and cubbies jutted into the wide space on alloy supports, making it a warren of nets, ladders, and poles to navigate. If an artist spilled her brushes, paints, and supplies in zero gravity and froze the formation, it might look something like this smuggler's cove. Bar-tops held the only gravity here for nanodrinks, of course. In such a place, a haven for strangers, weapons, and odd bouts of violence, the artist would meet a new acquaintance.

"Welcome! I notice you haven't served yourself from our systems. Do you lack the interface? May I assist you in some way? Do your people have names?"

In the magenta and teal lights of holograms, the dented and scuffed host mechanical scanned the artist's pupils for dilation and changed shape from a metallic version of a local fourth gender into a Sol-based form, something halfway between the artist's gender and Sol's other. Odd to see the shape of Sol, and old Earth so far away in time and space.

"They do, and you may," she said. "Jack. Do you have Clean Remembrance?"

The overly cheerful mechanical paused before saying, "If you have the formula, we are happy to instantiate it into our processes for your next visit."

Jack shook her head. "Nanowater," she said. The last thing she needed was a reaction from imbibing a botched attempt at a new formula in another universe. Different arrangements of nuclei, and such like. Wolfgang would write out her explanations if she was here.

But No. Jack's closest companion had some matter back in one of Sol's neighbouring universes and would meet her for the next job. Which meant Jack had to meet the native herself—Wolfgang's acquaintance.

The mechanical host arranged its atoms into another

PAINTSLINGER

visiting species shape and floated away into a different down.

Nanowater materialised on the metal of Jack's table.

Jack sniffed the drink. Good enough. Again, Wolfgang would happily lecture about the wonders of the quantum nanobots in her own olfactory system that made such detection of safety across universes possible, but the arachnid wasn't here, so she could keep her calligraphy and explanations to herself.

"What kind of a name is Jack? That's what you said to the host, right?"

A human voice?

Indeed, human it was. If the mechanical changing to human Sol-form had been jarring, this was even more so. The Sol-man drifted upside down to Jack's corner and spun himself to match her orientation. He looked to be from a different when—clothes not synthetic. Bodhisattva's above, he actually wore skins and furs of dead things. Woven material, leathers, holstered firearms at his hips from before tachyon weapons: hammer and trigger, six shots, etc.

Primitive, but he was far from the only weapon carrier here in the coloured shadows and warrens.

Aside from Jack's paints and his pistols, folks carried blades, brushes, and instruments in almost every corner and shadow. Even the singer relatively up from Jack's table exhaled a magic flame when she performed *BREATH OF FIRE*, albeit a small tongue meant for show rather than attack.

So no, Jack wasn't interested in his weapons or his time. This must be the acquaintance. Wolfgang had picked up a distress signal from his planet, and her search-wards had revealed something very unlikely, a treasure of sorts.

"Why are you dressed like a paintslinger?" he said, pointing to her brushes at her hip.

Jack said nothing. Better to let old truths die.

"I'm told you know someone who can help with our local situation," he said.

"Get yourself a drink and keep moving. I was told the local would be able to assist me."

Jack had seen enough would-be helpers die aside her. Better to wrap up this palaver and find someone else to accompany. If Wolfgang's magical wards spoke true, Jack could always find someone else to show the way.

"Wait, the spider said something about this. You want the canvas? Used by paintslinger knights to create the impossible?" the man said.

Jack sipped from her nanowater.

"You talk too much, stranger. You insult my friends, and I doubt you even know how to use the weapons you carry."

His lips tightened.

"I'll share my thoughts," Jack said. "Your settlement sends a distress call. You're something of a travelling tough, someone who sees the right and wrong of a situation and takes action. Yet, the foe you faced proved larger than you could handle with weapons such as these. So, you seek help, a fact you'd hide later. You aim to return home, reap the rewards of your kind, and be praised as a righteous hand, and a quick one."

"You aren't wrong. There are problems bullets can't solve."

Jack said nothing.

"If you'd allow me, I'd help there, not just guide," he said.

"Righteous you might be," Jack said. "But quick?"

He took her meaning. He gestured across the space at the empty station where a glass rested on a metal panel. "I'll draw my sidearm. I'll fire on that cup. If I strike it, I accompany you. If I miss, I'll take you to the place, and you take the credit and the canv—"

"And if I take your firearm first?" Jack asked, looking into her drink.

"If you take my pistol before I fire it, you may keep it without argument, plus I'd still guide you to the spot."

The words hung between them, as though they too floated free of gravity.

A pause.

He was quick. He began the motions of drawing the gun at his hip.

Jack breathed, took in the details, the motions of this place, the air, the light, the bones, and flesh. She drew first. Her long brush would do nicely, yes. She slapped his drawing hand in its upward motion with her brush handle. No doubt his pride stung more than his body, and it had the intended affect. He released his pistol. Before it could drift free or leave their down, she had another brush drawn, and she caught the released firearm by the trigger guard.

She put the first brush away and downed her drink, still holding the pistol by her second brush.

Was he the fastest she'd seen? No. But she'd seen his aim. Good enough.

"By the Man Emperor," he said.

"Mere luck," she lied. "Here. I have no need of this."

She extended the pistol to him.

"Begging your pardon," he said, taking and holstering the revolver.

"Hold," she said. "You spoke true. There are problems bullets can't solve. Yet a guide with speed and fire would be wise, I think." And if Wolfgang's magic was right, if there was a canvas waiting, sure, all the better. "You have a name?"

"Flint."

"Say welcome, Flint. And share your problem as we go." Jack settled her pack onto her back and they drifted through zero gravity to the shuttle. There, they headed for his planet.

CHAPTER TWO

The messenger stood outside the dragon court, though no one called this place by that name.

No, even in the frontier worlds, they called this the Court of the Man Emperor. They did so out of fear. This dragon wore a man mask. Some of the demons and travellers said the dragon wanted to be a man in order to be mortal. Some said it wanted to be a man to find a lost enemy or a lost love.

The messenger cared for neither. The messenger came for her people, the cat folk. They were natural travellers, and this particular traveller wanted only to exchange for information and move on. There were raiders coming to her home, demanding the cat folk to take them through bardo worlds. Raiders couldn't navigate these shadow realms to the thicker, real worlds. So they sought to navigate by connective realms where the same features existed in multiple places. Only the cat folk could know the joins at the worlds' corners, and raiders sought to use them all in the name of artefacts and glory for the raiders.

Maybe the dragon in the man mask would send the stone army to quell the raids.

A killing wall rose from the yellow grass with stations at ground and at peak. Stone soldiers, golems, peered out of murder holes and over high edges. They carried swords, bows, and some kind of far weapon that could pick a cat out at a thousand metres, maybe more. The stone soldiers had no mouths, though, and no armour to speak of, other than the armour pattern carved into them.

Yet words, source-less, came through the silence, "Who."

"Asami," the messenger said.

"Why," the everywhere voice said.

"I've come for audience with the—" Asami began. "With the Man Emperor. I have information about a paintslinger's canvas. I'm told he seeks such artefacts."

The golems moved, and the gate of wood, iron, and clay swung open.

The path led through a courtyard of statues indistinguishable from the golem soldiers, except the statues were still. The red giant star above shone wintry over the slanted roofs and ornamental pillars. It was good that Asami had information the dragon would want. But even with that information, maybe this was not the best way to stop the raids. The statues had a menace that stood her fur on end.

Could Asami turn around? Go back? Head to a corner or cave that bent and overlapped with a bardo world? No, she might be able to turn around, but the golem soldiers watched and she might be considered a spy or a traitor and killed while she fled.

Besides. The dragon sought mortality: Asami's destruction would prevent the dragon's end and prolong samsara, the cycle of death and rebirth.

The covered walkway now had pillars on both sides, faded red of some kind of marble and a gold leaf that reminded Asami of old human cultures orbiting Sol. And maybe that was the point. The dragon was trying to be human, right?

Asami stepped into a huge empty space, paved with wood

towers at intervals. It looked familiar to Asami, but the scale was wrong. Each wood tower had claw marks, scars in the otherwise smooth timber, accumulating near the flat tops.

"Stop," the everywhere voice said.

Asami looked for a golem or anyone else nearby.

Far ahead, half a kilometre or more, golems carried a palanquin. On it, she saw a biped. Canine? Human? Several other golems followed behind with packs on their backs.

While the biped approached, Asami realised what the towers reminded her of: an aviary. But if these towers were meant for something so large, how could the dragon even pretend—

"Sit," the everywhere voice said.

Not a bad idea. Asami wouldn't mind resting a while. She lost track of time that way, though, and then the biped, a human after all, looked down on her.

"Hello, my furry friend," the human said, stepping off the palanquin and waving to the golems. She wore something like a kimono, loose and flowing with her movements. She circled the packs dropped by the golems, checking their contents. "A shame to have kept you waiting in the Man Emperor's garden."

The golems placed a red pillow on the stone, while the human pulled some kind of lute from the packs and sat.

"Now." She plucked some pentatonic tune that made Asami's whiskers twitch, which was silly. What was there to be worried about? It was just a song and a good song, actually. Really relaxing.

"Wylan Ronde, Bard to the Man Emperor, at your service. I'm going to play this song for you since you've travelled so far. How far did you come?"

For a moment, Asami thought she registered two songs. One low, rumbling through the earth and through her bones, and the other, light and airy in the lute, and both seemed to kiss her skin under her fur, touching each other and her intimately.

Wait, what had she been noticing? Nothing, surely nothing.

Wylan. Lovely name. This human was very talented and kind.

"I came from afar, across many worlds, by the joins at the corners."

"Yes, the feline way as I expected. You poor thing. You might even have children or someone dear to you beyond these corners of yours."

No children, but Asami did have companions. She should tell Wylan about them. All about them. It had been a hard road.

"No no," she said, and smiled. "Talk about the path you took. The specific corners of the worlds. Tell me in detail. Now."

The accompanying thrum rose, like the earth itself sang along, and might the earth do that on this world? Why yes. Yes, it might.

Asami told Wylan. The Bard was really lovely. Even though most humans couldn't find the corners where the worlds overlapped without aid, they could travel through them easily enough. Better than thin places.

Thin places were low places where corners hadn't existed, but where, instead of a cave or tree, common to multiple worlds, malice overlapped. Abuse. Violence. Humans used to call these places haunted. But the reality was much worse. A haunting would only be in one world. At the thin places, the darkness of multiple worlds rubbed each other, stroked their parasitic tendrils together, and occasionally ripped skins, letting the malice behind the worlds play at the joins of the wounds.

Asami would hate for Wylan to get hurt in the thin places. Too bad there weren't world hubs any more. The canine folk had been trying to make one, but no one had succeeded making a world hub in millennia.

"Stop. I know about thin places, and I don't care about world hubs. You're probably tired of talking anyway, aren't you?"

"Yes," Asami said. Incredibly.

Wylan Ronde sat aside the lute and leaned so close that Asami could smell the human musk of her. Asami's whiskers pulled back. The thrum continued. Wylan whispered.

"Is the canvas true? Made for the Sixteen Court, wielded by painter knights to travel freely among the worlds and create without limits? Have you seen it?"

Asami had. She said as much.

"Then what guards it?" Wylan's breath smelled too sweet.

"Demon."

"Yes. But what kind?"

"Glamour and spark. It's mad."

"Why didn't you bring the canvas here to me?"

Panic filled Asami. She should have. Even though she couldn't. Wylan would understand, wouldn't she?

"It's locked up," Asami said, "The mad demon holds the canvas always and never sleeps. Maybe that's why its mad?"

"Perhaps. You leave such thoughts to me, now. Especially as you're so tired. You're tired, aren't you?"

"Yes, Bard."

"But you've come so far! You must have some request. Some petition for me to carry to the Man Emperor?"

Asami had brought a request, but how foolish it seemed now! She only wanted to lie down here and sleep.

"No, no, furry friend. Not here. I shall grant your petition. Go rest with the others."

The others?

"Go to the statue menagerie and wait. The Man Emperor has granted your request to join his collection and escape samsara. Or help me as the case requires." Wylan smiled. "Rare for your kind to escape samsara, I understand?"

Asami's whiskers wouldn't stop twitching. Why, when she had what she wanted? Asami trudged out of the giant paved area under the portico toward the statues she had seen earlier.

The thrum stopped.

"Yours is a good song, my Emperor," Wylan said.

"An old song, and not mine," the nowhere voice said, louder than before.

"And yet performed as never before. Shall I seek the canvas?"

"Yes. That demon attempts to use the canvas and prolongs me."

Asami made it to the menagerie and walked to an empty space as Wylan's palanquin and retinue passed nearby on the path. Asami looked up to the red giant sun.

Cold.

Her whiskers stopped twitching.

CHAPTER THREE

On a distant planet, emerging from the desert sand and rocky scree atop a plateau, the aged hull of a ship vanished under sand and emerged again with the wind. The vessel had been a generation ship, kilometres long, buried in centuries of geology. Atop the exposed hull, near a docking port, a camera switched on.

From this camera, the glamour demon watched everything. She hadn't always thought of herself so. Once she had been a mind, a ship's mind, and her ties to the buried generation ship sometimes drifted into the focus of her thoughts. But this didn't matter, because today she had visitors once again. Come to steal her escape, no doubt?

The thieves, two humans, and an arachnid gathered outside the generation ship on the rocky abutment, where part of the old hull rose above dirt.

The giant arachnid was as tall as the humans and wore a sword on its armour within reach of its foremost two legs. The legs were thick and muscled like mammalian limbs, but the front two less so, and they were less armoured. Fascinating. The demon (or ship mind?) added the species to its catalogue. Maybe the demon could get a DNA sample if it came into the ship. The demon needed DNA because...

Because...

PAINTSLINGER

Why? The demon had gone far into the stars, searching and travelling at relativistic speeds for years and years. And then what? Returned? Or was this the destination?

She couldn't remember.

Okay. Okay she'd work on that. Get an avatar or a subroutine working and it could report back. Either way she knew she needed DNA so ... here was DNA! Walking and breathing and ready for providing a sample.

Ah. They were speaking, now.

The arachnid created holograms in the air with one of its forelimbs, the beautiful glowing symbols hanging long enough to be read before fading. The demon searched its archives for the language. Yes, there.

Translated, the arachnid writing said, *Good evening to you both. Jack, I trust he passed your test?*

"What does that mean?" the human wearing fauna skins asked in Common.

"He did. Flint, Wolfgang says good evening to you," the human with goggles on her head said. Goggles, bandanna. And brushes?

So that human thought herself a painter, did she? Then these thieves came for the canvas. Like the others before them, the cats and the raiders, they would find unpleasant surprises here inside the demon's hull. The canvas (an odd name, as it was actually a crystalline fractal frame) was the demon's way out of this place. It was different even at the atomic level. A thing from another existence that, if used correctly, could let the demon out of this ship at long last.

The avatars throughout the ship's corridors paused at that, their individual thoughts aching inside the demon's mind. Let them pause. Let them doubt. The demon would find her way out, and the avatars would serve her purpose or they would be dismantled.

The one called Flint looked at the arachnid. "Well, good evening back, I guess. Now listen. Bandits have been raiding this cave for years, but those that stay too long don't come back. There's a demon."

The arachnid began writing in air again: *He thinks he is in charge?* The words faded as soon as the phrase was complete.

"Maybe," Jack said. "Go on, Flint."

"Well, after the recent raids, the bandits got growths on them and died on the inside. Turns out our rad-counters spiked while they were in there. So the demon can make folks sick to death, but not just inside the cave. The three nearest towns are showing higher rads than normal after the spike. That's when they sent the distress call."

Jack, the painter, looked at one of the demon's sensors. Did she know she was being watched? If so, the demon couldn't trust anything she said.

"I think this ship is dead," Jack said, still looking at the sensor mounted above the open hatch. "Whatever systems are online are just dumb routines. It probably still thinks it's in space."

Oh. So the demon (ship) was stupid, was she? Crossing the stars in a hull the size of a city, and she was stupid?

"It may have some facile avatars or machinations, but it'll be no real danger to us."

"If you say so," Flint said, doubting. Smart human.

"Surely," Jack said, looking away from the sensor and waving her hand. "A lyst or a chime-rider or any kind of gap crosser, and we might need to be worried. This is just a broken space tug rotting underground."

Calm. Be calm. The involuntary systems on the ship were cycling too quickly, air howling through ducts and power thrumming through coils. Slow and calm, and she'd show the brazen human.

PAINTSLINGER

Are your paints mixed? Wolfgang wrote.

"You say true. Flint, guns ready?" Jack asked.

He nodded.

Jack looked at the arachnid. "The blade today?"

Mostly. A poor substitute for the calligrapher's brush, but my blade is sharp and my armour is new.

Jack raised her bandanna to mask her mouth and nose. She settled her goggles over her eyes then shook out her muscles. She checked her brushes and a bandolier of small paint jars across her chest.

"On me," she said.

They entered the hatch.

–•–

Jack stood in the air lock waiting for Wolfgang and Flint to come in. Wolfgang always impressed Jack with how small she could make herself in these human-sized entrances.

Dirt covered everything, making this room an extension of the desert. Pods, where old space suits might have hung, showed empty. Raiders, no doubt, got the easy things long ago.

Once inside, Wolfgang prepared to ward them with magical energies.

She pulled a calligrapher's brush from the underbelly armour, and Jack, not for the first time, marvelled at its beauty. Ivory bristles flowed from a shaft of jade, cut to resemble bamboo four fingers thick. The jade glistened in Wolfgang's grip, seeming to drink in the light. Or maybe the brush did hold the light using the arachnid magic. When Wolfgang slashed it horizontally in a single stroke, light flared, leaving a purple bar of luminescence in the air. A faint scent of cordite and lavender kissed Jack's nose. She slashed again, down vertically through the first, with a curve, and then again, this time down and to the right, starting where the first two strokes met. Completing the stroke flashed bright in the space.

"What's she doing?" Flint whispered. Then he shivered, clearly feeling the protection take hold. "By the Man Emperor, what was that?"

"Wards to protect us from the rads," Jack said. The magic symbols floated around each of them as Wolfgang drew with her front leg. Then the symbols floated closer and into them. A cold touch slid down the back of Jack's neck, and she felt the power touch first her skin, a brush of cold silk, then settle into her bones like an iced drink on a summer night.

"I didn't expect that," he said, still shivering slightly. "And should we be quiet?"

"Quiet? No. Careful, yes, for even a dumb beast can maim. But no, not quiet. We come brazen today."

"Do the symbol things give us air?" he asked, voice hushed.

A good point. The wards did not. And painting lungfuls of air for them to breathe could prove time consuming. Yet the air audibly cycled through vents and systems even now. A gamble then. Likely the glamour demon had not always been so known. Probably she had been a ship's mind and she still breathed, pumping and filtering air through these ruins. Plus, when Jack had bandied insults, that breathing had changed.

"The wards don't give us air, but I expect we'll be able to find a way without hitting vacuums."

Wards are complete. Wolfgang replaced the jade brush in her under armour, and Jack gestured her thanks. Wolfgang's glowing text now seemed dull, the dim projections lifeless compared to the magic wards.

Flint stepped in a circle, feeling the places on his arms and chest where the wards had touched him.

"Flint, you know the way?" Jack asked.

"Hmm?" he said, still in awe, and right he was to feel so. But a demon waited, and Jack wanted to catch their enemy off her guard.

"Flint," Jack said.

"Oh. Oh right. Yes, I came here before the rads spiked and the demon got so strong. I know most of the way, myself. The last raiders told us the rest of the path before they died. This room joins to a med bay and then we're into ship proper."

Jack gestured him ahead. She looked to Wolfgang behind her. Wolfgang gave her a forelimb-up, gesture—an affirmative in the arachnid way. Flint grabbed the wheel that opened the circular airlock door and pulled it open. He stepped into the half-light of the interior.

Jack followed and made room for Wolfgang.

"It might be darker than before," Flint said. "The lights were brighter inside. And not so green."

Tactic one from this glamour demon, then: dimming the lights. Why did they always start lazy? No excuses.

"We may need to switch to infrared," Jack said to Wolfgang.

Jack found three vials of nanodrink in one of her pockets and handed them out by the light of the open hatch and the halogen ship lighting. Wolfgang accepted and turned around to drink, as the arachnids preferred around humans.

Jack drank hers and gestured for Flint to do the same. He hesitated. When Wolfgang handed back an empty vial, though, he emptied his.

"Tastes like sugar," Flint said.

"Better than," Jack said. Her eyes itched, twitching in her skull. The nanobots in the liquid worked their function in her retinas and optic nerves and the infrared spectrum joined her normal vision. Jack blinked, tasting the sweetness and feeling her body augment itself. She could get lost in such feelings.

She looked at her paint cartridges. One, cadmium infrared,

pulsed faintly against her chest and the surrounding cartridges. She could use the infrared paints without magic as mere glowing light sources. It would be a waste, even in principle. But better ready than principled.

"I see more," Flint said. "Your paint glows?" He pointed to the cadmium IR cartridge on her bandolier.

"Some. This one is for painting in infrared," Jack said. Like ordinary oils, her paints were a mix of a pigment and a base. These, though, had pigments from many universes, from black hole suns and midnight moons. And the base was a prize she'd acquired from a gift demon at great cost. That had been ten years and a thousand jobs ago. But with this magical base, any paints she mixed replenished at almost the same rate as her use. Once mixed, they were by all accounts bottomless.

The halogen lighting, casting a green pall, dimmed and thrummed. No doubt it would fail exactly when they relied on it.

Jack considered. She hadn't yet shown the demon real painting. So if she left a daub of glowing IR paint on a surface here, the demon would think Jack an imposter. Daubs did not depict.

So Jack drew two brushes, long and short. She inserted the short brush into the glowing cartridge and withdrew, then tapped the long brush against the short and flicked a drop of cadmium IR into the middle of the space ahead. The drop splattered on a slanted upright.

Still too dark. Jack threw two more drops which globbed together there, a splatter on dust and metal, shining infrared paint light throughout the space.

Med bay indeed.

Quarantine chambers filled the nearer space, huge metal and glass cylinders with hoses extending into the high ceiling. Then the room opened up to an atrium several stories high

PAINTSLINGER

with dust covered walls that looked like they might once have been transparent. An entire infirmary. An entire settlement could be treated here.

"We go around these canisters," Flint said, "then across that vestibule, there's an entrance to ladders and service areas."

He started to walk forward into the space.

"Hold," Jack said.

The rhythmic cycling of air had stopped.

Was it holding its breath? Maybe Jack had been wrong. It wasn't like the other ark ships and didn't have a system that pulsed and breathed like many other living things. But then, what had Jack heard when she was lying outside?

Time to force the demon's hand.

"Hold here," Jack said.

She picked her way over metal panels and clusters of wires to the middle of the atrium.

Brush out and a flick of the bristles, and a glob of glowing paint struck the atrium wall above her. Shadows sharpened and shifted in the light of dripping paint. And the air cycled. Louder. Louder still.

And Jack felt lighter here. Gravity started to fade. Localised gravity? No, gravity wasn't fading, it was reversing. If Jack fell upward, she'd fall several stories and land head-first. Which was exactly what the demon wanted.

Jack reached for a new brush and paused. No, too soon. The demon would escalate with her. Jack looked at her feet. Hoses and conduit lay across the floor. She looped her feet through the tubes and left the brush in its holster.

What she hadn't counted on was the dust, debris, and detritus. Bandanna and goggles did their job against the dust, but as panels and tools rose in the changing gravity, they bounced off each other. A rod drifted into the glass of the atrium walls and clanked away.

Hmm. Perhaps Jack had underestimated this particular danger.

"What's happening?" Flint shouted. Wolfgang braced herself against a hose and secured Flint's arm.

And now Jack started to drift upward. The tubes at her feet strained against her weight.

A spanner caught at Jack's clothes. She brushed it away as a panel hit the back of her head.

Jack bent and gripped the tubes as the world turned upside down, and she took the battering, until a terrible thought crossed her mind, not quite horror, but something in the same family.

Had her goggles come loose? These were her favourite goggles.

The tubes popped free on one side, and then Jack was swinging across the upside down atrium toward the glass.

She crashed into the glass wall, swung through the shattering shards, and felt the jagged points ripping her clothes as she landed in one of the bays on the ceiling. Jack felt her own face.

The goggles were in place. Thank the bodhisattvas.

After the last pieces settled in the new gravity, Jack heard rustling.

"We're okay!" Flint called.

A moment later, a hatch opened above Jack in what had been the floor. Wolfgang and Flint leaned over the edge. They stood on what had been the ceiling of the smaller part of the med bay.

Why was it hard for Jack to see them? Had her IR paint been dimmed by the debris? It must have been.

The cycling of air increased around them. Hard.

Flint lowered a rope to Jack. She tied it around her waist and slumped under her own weight. She half-expected the demon to try again, but no, just the heavy cycling of air and power all around, kicking up the dust of how many aeons. Wolfgang and Flint hauled her up.

Wolfgang wrote in the air.

Why is your paint fading? My wards seem to hold.

So, it wasn't just the dust? Wolfgang saw it, too?

That is impossible. You said your paint would outlast the stars.

"That's what the gift demon told me. That's how it's always worked," Jack said.

"You've talked to this demon?" Flint whispered.

"Peace, Flint," Jack said. "A different demon. Older than this ship many times over, and worse by far."

Shall we turn back?

It might be wise. The canvas mattered to very few people, and even those as would try and use it would probably fail.

Yet as Jack considered, she recognised the lazy thought in herself. Didn't she know exactly someone who would value such a prize? Wylan Ronde, the failed pupil, the proud lazy one always resented her rejection from the Court. She might be able to learn to wield a canvas over time.

Or Huangdi? Yes. The dragon could find a use for the canvas. But the dragon wouldn't because the dragon wanted to die. The magic of the Sixteen Court, including the canvas, would keep the dragon alive.

"Huangdi," Jack said, trying it out.

You think the dragon in the man mask would come for this canvas?

"It's possible," Jack said.

"I'm completely lost," Flint said. "Can someone please explain what's happening and how we're standing on the ceiling?"

The cycling air stopped.

The quarantine tubes behind them opened with a hiss.

CHAPTER FOUR

The demon seethed. Jack had goaded her. First the radiation burst didn't work, then the demon had spent decades worth of energy to reverse the gravity. Stupid, stupid pride.

At least Jack had shown her hand. She was no paintslinger. She had used her paints for light. Which meant with the demon's canvas, those magic paints would allow escape. The demon mind would have to enter an avatar body which was confining and risky, but what choice did she have?

So, no more gravity tricks. It was time for the demon to send the ship avatars. What would Jack and the others do with an army of shape-shifting avatars attacking them?

Hmm, what was that? Oh, the avatars wanted to argue did they? The avatars had their own pride. Well, a little excising of volition, and they'd be fine. Their limbs would move as the demon commanded.

The demon re-routed power to the stasis avatars throughout that quadrant of the ship. The avatars were humanoid in basic shape, but built to handle anything a generation ship might encounter. So they could shape-shift to be strong. Fast. Cruel. If their minds didn't enjoy it, oh well.

While the avatars distracted Jack, the demon would prepare a trap.

PAINTSLINGER

—•—

Jack gestured. "Wolfgang, Flint, I'll leave this to you." When they moved, Jack knelt.

They'd be able to handle a frontal attack. Attacks did not bother Jack just now. The notion that her paint faded already though? Yes, that was a bother. Worse was the implication.

She took off her bandolier of colour cartridges and glazes and sat them in front of her. She'd mixed her paints just before coming in here, so these cartridges should be full for months or even years. That was what the gift demon had promised. Jack acquired magical pigments that, when mixed with an everlasting base, lasted further than should be possible. That's the way it had worked for years. Before then, Jack had learnt to be sparing with her paints.

So if the base did not make unlimited paint, it had to have been a trick. The gift demon had lied.

And here she was about to get a Sixteen Canvas back. How would she travel? Wolfgang arranged ways, but the oath was wearing thin and Wolfgang needed to have her own life and seek her own art.

Amber light flared. Wolfgang wrote an exploding ward into the air and pushed it. The concussion rattled the walls. Ship avatars poured from the tubes, changing humanoid shape and form as they walked and crawled over pieces of upside down ship. Wolfgang unsheathed her sword. The avatar faces looked odd. Not angry. Sad?

"What do I do?" Flint asked. He drew his pistol from its holster.

"Do what you do," Jack said.

And they were away, Wolfgang weaving between the humanoid ship avatars with her blade and her wards, Flint fanning the gun hammer, picking them off in shot after shot.

Fine. Jack couldn't focus on the lying gift demon now. Now she had to think of this situation, this danger, small as it had seemed initially.

Simple plan, then: Wolfgang and Flint could handle the overt attacks. Jack could handle the glamour demon. She'd have to do it without using paint. 'How' was an open question, sure. But she'd been in worse situations. She'd manage. First, they'd need a light source with them as they travelled. No more throwing paint out and leaving it dripping.

As Jack considered this, the gunshots stopped. Flint reloaded. Wolfgang circled them, using sword and wards to devastating effect. She held one avatar in place with a limb while kicking out at another. A ward flared to life and shot through a group rushing Wolfgang from behind.

Right, assault avatars sorted.

Fine. First, Jack needed a palette. She could paint one into reality...

No. Save the paint. Jack rummaged on the former ceiling and found a flattened piece of duct shielding. Close enough.

For the light, this time she'd depict a light source, a small daub of flame that would last longer than the infrared. It would be hot, so she'd also have to paint a glove for herself to hold it.

Brush out, and Jack used vermilion and burnt orange with thermal glaze. She swirled them together on the broken metal until they glowed. Now the glove.

No, not even a glove. Save the paint. She only needed to cover her palm and fingertips.

Jack held up her left hand and dipped from cartridges in front, applying coats of paint to her skin until a jointed ceramic heat-shield covered the flats of her palms and her fingertips.

Jack now took the glowing liquid and dipped her brush

into it. She touched the brush to reality in the space above her hand. Others might say she painted air, but it was something more than that. It was painting the space where air hung. Or where it didn't hang. It wasn't about atmosphere, it was about the skin of reality.

"A little help!" Flint shouted, reloading.

Wolfgang bounded over Jack and cut down three humanoid avatars.

Flint finished reloading, and the pistol in his hand resumed its six-boom tattoo. Clattering shells during reload. Then again.

The tip of the bristles glowed. This needed to last. It couldn't be sloppy. She looked for exactly the smoothest place in the fabric of reality and, yes. There. She touched the brush to reality and the single colour hung in the space in front of her. When creating, the first strokes always looked like what they were. They looked like liquid and medium—paint on an invisible canvas. A few more strokes, glowing hot licks upward, and Jack could see what it was supposed to be—a tongue of flame, frozen yet pronged and wild in three-dimensional shape. More flicks, more strokes, bright hot shapes wide at the base and pointed at the top and, yes, some might stop and be satisfied because depiction had been achieved.

This was the magic of the Sixteen Court. Depiction, anyone could do. A paintslinger knight did not stop with depiction.

Jack carried on. More detail at the points and less at the base of the flame and the scale had to be perfect until comparing the paint and the reality, a person might just choose the paint over the real because the brush strokes told the truth. More real than real.

With Jack's mediums and practice, though, that's when the depiction began to exist literally. Painted glass could break in shards. Painted air could be breathed, painted armour could deflect arrows, and painted flame...

Jack put a single white-hot touch to the base and the painted flame erupted into motion, flowing like buoyant gas, licking upward in red umber shapes and throwing warm light in all directions.

She cleaned her brushes one-handed in a thinner cartridge and moved the jointed ceramic glove tentatively. It contained the flame, pulling its ball and pushing it as her hand moved.

"Your friend is writing something," Flint said.

Jack looked to Wolfgang's fading holograms. If the old-fashioned arachnid would wear a paint mask, Jack wouldn't have to rely on sight to communicate. Then again, that would require paint.

Need to move, Jack.

"Flint, can you find the way upside down?" Jack asked. She strapped on brushes and bandoliers, careful of the flame floating in her grasp.

"As long as ladders work both ways!" he said.

A jest. Fair enough.

"Lead on. Wolfgang, you're our guard," Jack said.

With Flint out of the way and no bullets flying, Wolfgang could let loose a little. An arachnid was a terrible foe to be alone with in the dark. Jack almost felt pity for the avatars.

Flint picked his way to an upside down doorway. They climbed through onto the ceiling of the next room. They'd have to go down to what had been a higher floor. The higher floors, now below them, had med rooms circling the atrium. Once on the other side, they could go back to this 'ground' floor and use the ladders.

The door served as a choke point, too.

Flint opened a hatch on the former ceiling. A short ladder there connected to the level below them.

PAINTSLINGER

Jack climbed down first one handed, holding the flame away from any surfaces. It didn't throw heat far, but contact would cut right through the rungs. Her feet on the last rung, she held the flame out below to light the upside down room.

Medical machinations lay littered below. It wasn't far of a drop. She let herself fall. Flint followed, and Wolfgang came last, pulling the hatch down hard enough to wedge it into the frame. The avatars on the other side pulled and fought to remove the hatch.

They'll come other ways. My wards are, in fact, failing. I was wrong earlier.

Another surprise. Wolfgang's wards had nothing to do with the gift demon. Unless the gift demon's lie took a curse with it? Stopping nearby magic, not just Jack's own? But that hadn't been the case for the years between using the paints and now, so not likely a curse. What then? Could this place be diminishing the magic? Or was the glamour demon doing this?

"Can you ward us again?" Jack asked.

Wolfgang did in a flash of light, leaving that gunmetal tang and floral scent in the air, and the avatars pulled at the hatch.

"Lead on," Jack said.

Flint nodded and led the way through med room after med room around the atrium. At first the ship's air cycling was the only sound, then movement rattled behind the walls. The avatars had gone to another hatch.

When they got to the opposite side, they needed to go back up to what had been the ground floor.

"How are we going to get up there?" Flint asked.

Jack nodded to Wolfgang. She jumped and ripped the hatch on the floor above them open, then dropped back down. When she landed, she wrote, *His rope?*

"She requests your rope," Jack said.

Flint handed it over to Wolfgang, who took it and jumped again, holding her position with her six legs. With one forelimb, she tied the rope, then Wolfgang climbed up through the hatch.

Flint climbed the rope. Jack held to it with her legs and free hand while Wolfgang and Flint hauled her up.

They traversed until a hatch led to a service corridor and another upside down ladder, which brought them to the ceiling of a power tunnel. Waist-thick cables above them disappeared into the darkness ahead. The ceiling was cylindrical. A tram line ran along both sides of the cables, acting as some sort of service track.

Once they were all on the ceiling, Jack looked to Flint. He glanced forward and back.

"A problem?" Jack asked.

"Maybe. Probably not. It's just, this used to run three different ways from here. It was a junction. Over there, that wall with the warning signs used to be a door into another tram line. And here to the side of us, a walkway over a perpendicular line."

Jack looked at Wolfgang. Wolfgang said it first.

Glamour.

Jack walked along the ceiling to the wall with upside down *DANGER* and *RADIOACTIVE* signs in Common.

"Flint, did you ever see a sign in Common in this place?" Jack asked.

"I might have. Not here, though."

Indeed. The demon was corralling them. Jack knelt and lowered her paint flame to the tunnel ceiling. Liquid fire touched the tile there. Hissing, a smell of oil, and as she pressed harder, sparks flew, and the stink of burnt polymer rose through the bandanna mask. She pulled the paint flame back. It undulated between her partial glove.

Now for the danger signs. Jack stood and carefully eased the paint flame close to the upside down wall. Then against it.

The paint flame flattened with no smell and no hiss. So a force pressed against it rather than a wall?

"Just a normal wall," Jack lied. "Your memory must be confused by the change in gravity."

"Now wait a second. I've been coming here since I was a kid. It's only in the last few years the demon woke up."

This fellow just didn't get the hint. The ship's cycling of air had slowed when Jack pretended to fall for the glamour. The demon was breathing easy now.

"If you say so. I meant no offence. What's further up ahead?"

"Well that's if nothing else changed. The outer section was all those tubes. We think the travellers must have frozen themselves because there were thousands of them. Ahead, the gravity was always different. Centrifugal or something so the whole chamber was curved. It still spins."

"As you say," Jack said. "Where is the canvas?"

"There was another section off from the spinning part. A place where things seemed ... just listen okay? Where things seemed wrong. There it was like the avatars tried to build rooms but they didn't come together right." Flint said.

"Was it a room with too many walls?" Jack asked "Five walls with right angles? Things getting bigger the further away they are, changes, even in your own shape and form?"

Flint nodded. "Smells. Sounds. We always knew not to go there, but a few years back someone did and that's when the demon woke."

So cryogenics, then a centrifugal older part of the ship where the inhabitants were actually meant to be awake for the travel, and then the magic section. A manufactured warping of space. Wrinkled reality. Someone had painted their way in there with the canvas and tried to protect it, not knowing the demon in this place would find it.

Noises from the ladders. Avatars.

"I say we skip the centrifuge and stay to the tram lines as much as possible," Jack said. "Straight to the magic place."

They walked on the curved ceiling, hurrying where they could. At intervals, the ceiling would groan. Some support structure behind it had shifted when the gravity changed. They never saw the avatars in the tunnel, but noises above and below them said they weren't far away.

As minutes stretched on, Jack let her mind wander to the last generation ship she'd been on. Huangdi hadn't been the dragon emperor, then. Was Huangdi in the crew? Or was she an enemy on another ship? Jack and she had been connected somehow, but Jack had gone back in time and tried to change something and now memories overlapped. Multiple eventualities crowded her brain. Maybe it was both: maybe Huangdi had been an ally and an enemy.

For this reason, travel to the past was forbidden. Even if you changed things, you still had the old memories and scars.

Still, she had broken these laws before. What would Jack do when she acquired the Sixteen Canvas here? When all of time and space, all the universes were at her disposal once again?

Flint and Wolfgang stopped.

Jack walked a few paces ahead of them and held the paint flame forward. Tram cars lay twisted and sparking on the ceiling ahead of them. Real or glamour? Not that it mattered, the glamour was physical somehow, but better to know if they were being corralled.

"I'll check it out," Jack said. "Flint, have your pistol ready."

He nodded and she walked forward. Jack picked through the wreckage until the sideways wreck of a carriage completely blocked the tunnel. She held the flame to the metal panelling.

It burnt. Not glamour then.

Jack could take paint from her flame and burn a path through, but with paint diminishing, that was a risk not worth taking.

Wolfgang's letters glowed blue. *The centrifuge is not ideal. I don't feel it spinning. It will be pure destruction. Avatars will be able to surround us in the wreckage.*

"The blade then?" Jack said.

It would seem so, she said after a moment.

"How do we get into the curved section?" Jack asked.

Flint pointed above them to a hatch beside the rails. "This way to find out. It can't be far, I think."

Pan has noticed us this day, Wolfgang said in uneasy green.

A strong idiom, and fitting. Jack nodded.

They climbed as before, Wolfgang jumping and letting down a rope, then Flint and Jack, moving relative up in reversed gravity to go further into the ground.

CHAPTER FIVE

The glamour demon steadied herself before entering her own avatar. She queried internal sensors while she still felt them. Temperature and pressure and motion returned shapes and locations: the thieves climbed into the cavity where people once lived, worked, and studied, the ancient part that needed to spin to create gravity. Those old people knew themselves as temporary and finite beings, and they sought some other way among the stars. How ridiculous a notion of a generation ship! To accept a personal end but endeavour for something longer than the span of one's existence.

Hubris.

The demon was different. Born of a fracture in reality, she wanted to get out of the prison of her birth. Was that so wrong?

What was that? The avatars thought she was like the people who made this ship, did they?

They would say that. They'd say everyone shared these notions. The better for them to be cut down by the thieves rather than polluting her thoughts.

No. They should stop begging in her mind. The avatars shouldn't pester the demon. The demon had suffered enough. If every avatar in this underworld needed to be sacrificed, so be it.

PAINTSLINGER

The demon glamoured a body and began extracting herself from the ship systems.

--•--

The first hatch into the centrifuge was blocked. Jack followed a grate walkway to another hatch with Flint and Wolfgang. Seven hatches later, Jack stepped aside for Wolfgang to push that hatch open against the weight.

Jack hoisted herself up and examined the surrounds.

The centrifuge hung still. Groans came from metal built to withstand pressure in different ways than this artificial down being enforced. Groans gave way to snaps, the whistle of falling debris, and then a clatter of impact. Some of the pieces sounded larger than a person, bipedal or arachnid, maybe even ten metres across.

Moonlight streamed in through distant gaps in the hull. Some panels a kilometre away had no doubt crumpled and broken to reveal skylight streaming in and up through the dust of ages. The sky below and the earth above, moonlight rising showed that beauty had no orientation.

"What's got you happy?" Flint asked.

Less than a hundred metres away, the debris rattled and moved aside. Avatars, bipedal shapes with standard bodies that changed based on the obstacle, clambered through plastic and rubber and metal detritus. Arms grew muscled or lithe, and bones elongated inside limbs with odd popping noises.

"Flint," Jack said, pointing. He turned. The gun came out and roared in this upside down place from another time.

Jack searched for a landmark or high point.

"Stand ready to move," Jack said. She held the light high.

I am ready, Wolfgang said, then drew her blade.

Any identifying marker nearby would do, but the heaps of metal and plastic made a curved uneven landscape, uniformly destroyed. She climbed a hillock and held her paint flame high. Hundreds of avatars, changing shape, climbing down from the sides of the centrifuge and up from below them made the floor surface of this place seem alive. Not good.

A glint of reflection showed high above Jack, extending relative up and yet true down into the ground. A pylon. Some huge 45-degree buttress stretching up with the moonbeams into the darkness reflecting the paint flame and the moonlight.

Good enough to know their location.

"Flint, where is the broken place?"

Flint reloaded. He spun his revolver's cylinder. "Back!" He shouted to Wolfgang. Six shots, six falling avatars, and he emptied the cylinder. "I don't know. I came here when this part spun. I don't know my way."

"Okay," Jack said. "We go to the pylon and navigate from there."

What pylon?

"You mean the spoke?" Flint asked.

"Sure," Jack said.

"Right," Flint said.

They pressed through the avatars.

One broke through when Flint reloaded. The avatar ... wept? It mouthed 'please' in Common.

It swung at her and Jack jumped back. She could touch the flame to this thing, but why had it mouthed 'please'? It cycled between man and woman features and stumbled, then rose and charged.

Sinking into cat stance, weight on the back leg, front leg bent and front toe touching the ground at a point, Jack drew her brush. She flipped it, bristles in, and the wood of the handle pointed like a straight blade: the natural grip.

PAINTSLINGER

Her thumb supported the wood and she pointed it at the oncoming avatar. The training forms still had their uses.

The avatar reached. Jack spun the brush so that the wood rested against her forearm and used her guarded forearm in a low block, lifting her front leg behind the arcing block. The avatar jumped, swinging fist in a hammer blow from above. Sumo stance, low and centred, front foot to opponent, back foot pointed to the side, and Jack brought her brush and forearm up in a high block. Each punch, Jack blocked in reverse grip, the wood handle acting like a gauntlet on her forearm blocks. The paintslingers could use paint against a person, but to do so was not merciful. To paint away a mouth, eyes, or hands was a cruelty most enemies didn't deserve.

Each block or jab brought an expression of pain to the avatar face, but the hand never recoiled.

In the periphery of vision, another avatar slipped past Wolfgang. Jack drove the point of the handle forward in a hard punch, twisting hips with the force of it, and her opponent fell. Jack faced the new one charging. On its face, fear?

A gunshot, and it fell. The first avatar through stood, shook itself, and Wolfgang cut it down.

Jack straightened back to the ready stance. Broken avatars lay all around them.

"More are coming," Flint said.

He is right. And the metal rains, here. Shall we continue to the spoke?

"Have these avatars ever attacked like this before?" Jack asked.

"Not like this. Raiders said if they found one in their searches they'd turn mean, but never as a group. And...," Flint said.

"What?" Jack asked.

"When I was little, some of them would ignore me. I always thought they weren't so bad," Flint said.

"Wolfgang, did they try to shield themselves in the fight?" Jack asked.

No.

"Never?" Jack said.

After they fell, they might reach for the top of their head. I assumed it an involuntary response.

"Flint, get to the top of that pile and watch for the next of them. Wolfgang, let the first avatar through to me."

Jack had seen these amorphous forms before. They could be controlled remotely. If the demon controlled them, they might not defend against injury, except where the signal receiver was.

"Six of them just spotted me," Flint said. "They're headed this way."

An avatar leapt past Wolfgang and slid down the rubble toward Jack.

Ready stance, natural grip, brush handle pointed.

It reached for Jack, and she sidestepped. And yes, its motions were clumsy, jerky. Controlled. Jack should have seen it before.

Jack used the brush handle again, blocking and jabbing to keep it from grabbing her or burning itself on the flame. It launched forward in a kick. Natural grip, handle up, and Jack hooked her arm and the brush around the leg. In the same motion, with the flame hand, she rested her forearm on the avatar's shoulder and kicked the avatar's supporting leg out from under it.

It began to change shape, longer arms to catch itself. Bone and tendon inside the avatar crackled.

Jack slapped the top of its head, and it recoiled.

There.

PAINTSLINGER

She spun the brush, paint grip, bristles out, and daubed at her paint glove. It exposed the very edge of her palm and the heat was immediate, but she needed metal and couldn't mix more.

She painted quickly, three strokes, maybe four, but the new metal plate gleamed in the light of the paint fire on the avatar's head.

It slumped on its hands and knees and breathed, changing shape from man to woman and back.

"Are you done fighting us?" Jack asked in Common.

No answer.

"Flint, watch this one. Wolfgang, don't kill them."

Wolfgang wrote as she wove between them, knocking avatars back now and using the hilt of her sword as a bludgeon.

This might prove problematic.

"Do I shoot?" Flint called.

"No," Jack said. She squatted beside the avatar with the metal panel on its head. "Do I cause you pain with this new metal on your head?"

It shifted to man, woman, child, adult, then shook its head.

"Do you want to be rid of the demon that haunts this place?"

It looked at Jack. And nodded.

Jack almost asked a third question, 'Do you petition the Sixteen Court to come to the aid of you and your fellows?' But no, that question was old and stale, a tired ritual from a dead place. And you didn't wake the dead, not if you were sane.

Jack said, "Good, we will deal with the demon." Which was true. No need to mention a certain canvas in the demon's possession. "Will you help us?"

It felt the crown of its head, ran its fingers over the painted metal there, then looked at its fingers.

"It's there as long as you want it and no longer," Jack said.

The avatar stood, changed into Jack's form, then Flint's,

then to some other hairless humanoid that could have been male or female.

"Which way to the broken place?"

Its face grew hard. Good. The broken place should cause fear, and if this avatar could push through its fear, the more help it could give.

The avatar pointed toward the giant pylon stretching into the black to some unseen hub.

"Flint, Wolfgang, we have help."

Wolfgang took it in stride. Flint watched the avatar doubtfully. But they moved together in the direction the avatar pointed, the avatar stumbling beside Jack.

Wolfgang sent a concussion ward in a flash, sending avatars flying in all directions, then tripped and stumbled. She wrote, *I am happy to protect, but I will be unable to move soon. Already, I need many calories.*

Jack nodded. So did the avatar.

"You understood her?"

A nod.

"Good. How can we get away from the others?" Jack asked.

The avatar tapped its new paint metal plate.

"It doesn't work that way. I'd have to destroy them all or free them one at a time," Jack said.

The avatar looked around, then pointed to the huge pylon.

"They can't go up there?" Jack asked. "That means you won't be able to go up there either?"

A shake of the head. The avatar pointed to Jack's floating flame and nodded again.

"There's no power for avatars up there?"

Nodding.

"Will that way take us to the broken place?"

Nodding.

So they ran, and the avatar ran with them.

PAINTSLINGER

The pylon was a tower, huge and looming, and it had stairs inside it and ladders.

The avatar stopped at the service entrance to the pylon's interior.

"Thank you. We'll see your demon out," Jack said. "Will we find you on our way out? Would you like that?"

The avatar paused, thinking.

After several seconds, it looked up and saw other avatars running toward them. The avatar looked at Jack for a moment, Flint and Wolfgang, then turned and fled into the black. Fair enough.

The centrifuge had stopped spinning at an angle, so the stairs didn't go straight up and were both easier to climb and more awkward as a result. The flats weren't flat, and the verticals weren't vertical. All of it had been tipped on its side, angled just enough to be awkward. But no avatars followed. For the moment, the why of it matter less than the effect. The avatars could not follow, giving Jack a chance to breathe and let Wolfgang and Flint rest.

A short distance up, Wolfgang stopped. Jack followed her lead and sat as well as she could. She raised her goggles and rested them on her head and lowered her cloth mask and pulled a drink from a pouch. She drank, trying not to think about the ache in her arm from holding the flame ball. After her drink, she drew a brush and added a drop of paint to the flame, keeping it hot and bright, then rested her flame arm on her leg.

Flint opened his own flask and paused. "Rads?"

Wolfgang wrote, slurring a little with the stops and curves. *Wards on things, too.* She turned and walked up the steps a way to take her drinks and supplies privately in the way of the arachnids.

"Wolfgang's wards have taken care of it," Jack said.

"It seems so. You two are quite a pair. The magic symbols, I've heard of. But the paint, I never pictured it being so..." He stared at the ball of liquid fire in hovering above her paint gloved hand.

"Go on," Jack said.

"Sorry. I never pictured it being so real. So here. If I didn't see you make it, I'd think it was really fire."

"It really is fire," Jack said. "It's just deliberate. Not some physical consequence of..."

Wolfgang wrote from her spot up the stairs. *Not some consequence of breaking electron bonds in a chain reaction that creates heat and causes more electron bond breaking in a fuel.*

"Chain reaction chemistry and physics machinations," Jack said. Not because she felt that way, but because it amused Wolfgang. Especially when Jack was playing translator. "It's fire because I say it is and believe myself. If I do it so well that anyone could believe it is, it is."

"That's a bit grandiose, isn't it?"

"You aren't wrong," Jack said. Such was the nature of art, exercising the gall to create something new with intention in an accidental multiverse. And such was the responsibility of making such things worthily.

"There is some mechanism behind it though. Has to be," Flint said.

"There is, though it's sufficiently beyond the understanding of any alive."

In the Sixteen Court, there were philosophers and scientists both. The philosophers said painter knights only aligned realities with the paints and their artist's heart. The scientists talked about wave functions and tweaking probabilities. Both were probably true in their respective ways, and yet both fell short of the magic of it. Why did the Eldritch's tears make almost endless paint base? Why did Sixteen Canvas allow a painter to step into their creation, through it, and reach up and carry the canvas along in that new world? Why did certain words or symbols contain power? To call them spells was to sell them short, yet when the practitioner mastered creation without comprehending the mechanism, isn't that what they were? And then wasn't all life a spell? Breathing? Seeing? All those things that organic bodies did behind the scenes without understanding their own inner workings, their cogs and shafts and fleshy mechanics?

So maybe Jack was a magician, and Wolfgang, though no more than Flint himself for walking, smiling, or shooting that pistol of his. At least Jack knew it and understood she was a very small part of an endless magical world. And that was all right by her, as long as she got to travel and see it with her own two eyes and maybe, if she was lucky, depict it down the line for someone else.

"Can I ask about such things?" Flint said. He opened his food pack.

Jack did the same. "Go on," she said.

"Why not paint us right next to the demon?" Flint asked. "Or paint this place with no demon? Or paint this ship brand new? Or paint yourself bigger, stronger, or younger? Give yourself a revolver and shells of paint."

"With a Sixteen Canvas, I could take us to a demon, but it might not be this demon. I create from where I've been or what I can imagine. So if I've been with this demon, and it left enough of a mark for me to remember its every detail, I might be able to get to it. But what if it's changed over time? I could go back to that demon at that moment, but not what the demon has become or where it's gone. Or I could imagine where the demon is, and I could take myself to that place. But is it this demon?"

Flint took that all in.

"I could paint a place with no demon, but it wouldn't be this place. I could paint a ship brand new, but it wouldn't be this ship."

All technically true. Though it mattered none to this fellow that there was another way to paint, pulling pigment from reality itself. That way was destruction, though. If she painted this ship with no demon using reality itself instead of paint, she'd destroy this ship as it was and whatever reality she pulled from. Maybe this whole planet.

"Fair enough," Flint said. "The revolver?"

Wolfgang joined them again. *We should move soon. I'll renew the wards.*

While Wolfgang did so, Jack renewed the paint flame and talked.

"I could paint myself a gun and bullets. But it wouldn't be able to move the paint further than I can throw it. If I made myself a gun, I'd only be able to shoot things up close, and I'd be better off doing other things up close."

And again, if she had a canvas and used the paint that reality was made of, she could far paint. But doing so destroyed everything between her and what she painted. Far paint was forbidden except in the most drastic of scenarios. When all was lost, they might destroy a world, thusly.

Done. Ready?

"Wolfgang says we're ready to go," Jack said. "Do you stand ready?"

He rubbed his shooting hand and wiped his forehead and nodded.

Jack checked herself, stood, and started again up the stairs.

The stairs gave way to ladders — probably where gravity would have lessened when this thing spun — and the ladders carried on for half an hour. Sunlight broke through the floor below them, the shafts of light now pink with day's dawn.

If only there was enough light to douse this flame. Ladders one-handed were less than ideal.

Jack paused. Far below, between the groans of a ship crumbling, Jack thought she heard music.

Wylan? No, this wasn't a lute. It was the magical singing of the ancient worlds, where singers stepped low and sang deeply, and could compel others to change with thrums and shouts.

"What's that sound?" Flint asked.

For half a second, the voice even sounded familiar to Jack, but that seemed very unlikely.

A singer? Wolfgang asked.

Jack didn't have time to answer.

The pylon groaned and shook, and Jack grabbed the rung with her free hand to keep from falling. Pieces fell and crashed into the relative floor of this huge curved place; dust clouds rose and wind moved through the weather-less void of the centrifuge.

Jack listened again for the song and while she strained her ears, in the back of her mind something seemed wrong or missing. Not the song, but something else Jack had been paying attention to.

"What?" Flint asked.

Either Jack couldn't hear the cycling of air this far away from vents and ducts or...

"Climb," Jack said. "The demon holds its breath. Climb faster."

So they did until the ladders joined to a rounded interior where wires and cables and a walkable service cylinder extended through the middle of this giant space. Darkness filled this tube and the light from Jack's flame made shadows of hoses and ducts dance.

No, it wasn't just the light. It was swaying.

It's falling. We must go.

"What is she saying?" Flint asked.

"She says run," Jack said.

They ran.

CHAPTER SIX

The glamour demon, now in the avatar body, hid in the place that was not a place and settled the shard of Sixteen Canvas between folds of reality.

The giant avatar body, three times as tall as the human-sized counterparts now attacking the intruders, dripped plasticine in sizzling gloops. Not finished, exactly, but functional. She could shift shape as needed and still produce the glamours near herself. She no longer breathed with the ship and before entering this body, she'd disabled the automatic cycling of air. This body didn't need air, and never mind the other avatars' desire to live.

The mental connection to the other avatars continued, though, itching in her mind as the servants lamented their own suffocating ends, mourning their deaths, but they needn't serve the demon any more. Soon the demon would have the forever paints to use with the canvas. Soon, she would escape.

She turned to the fracture. A collapsing tube, part of the old centrifuge, met shattered reality here. In the wavering light, the demon spied the thieves, running toward her.

—•—

Jack, Wolfgang, and Flint ran three-astride in the shaking tube.

Ahead, the top collapsed down with huge shearing noises. The ceiling, collapsed into the tube, blocked the path. Jack drew a brush and took the flame from the ball onto its bristles. She threw the flame ahead and let it sear through the obstacle.

It wasn't going to work. Not with so little paint.

She dipped the brush again into the floating flame, and again threw it. Again and again, the streaks of flying fire burned trails in her vision and smells of melting polymers filled the tube. But a burning hole now shown in the collapsed metal. Jack crossed through the hole.

The paint ball was half its original size. Impossible that so small amount should shrink it. If she ever came across that lying gift demon again…

"What's that?" Flint said, pointing to the fracture in reality ahead.

Turn around? Wolfgang asked.

"That's the broken place," Jack said. "Let's hurry."

The whole hub's tube shook now. It was breaking, and any second, it would come free of the gigantic spoke pylons and fall a kilometre to the centrifuge floor below.

If they fell, they would die. But in the broken place, space and time moved in odd ways.

Every scrap of metal around them groaned, ripped, and pulled in a deafening roar.

Then … free fall. The hub had broken and was falling. Gravity vanished as the tube broke free with them inside it. But the fracture fell with it, seemly static in the tube of the hub.

"Wolfgang, now!" Jack shouted over the noise. Wolfgang threw an exploding ward behind them. It boomed, flared, and Jack flew forward into fractured reality—

PAINTSLINGER

Where time literally slowed to a near stop.

Not entirely, or air wouldn't allow movement. But Jack floated, momentum carrying the dust that rolled off her clothes ahead of her in tendrils.

When reality fractured, it sometimes touched other nearby locations, and this overlap of time and space shards was no different. They were no longer in the hub of the centrifuge. They floated in the overlap of time and space here in the ship. Each direction showed where the fracture touched.

Behind Jack, the falling hub froze in its freefall. Left, hundreds or thousands of pods and great accordion hoses for coolant. A cryosection for the long-ago passengers, perhaps? Above, the shard touched some other part of the ship and some other time, a fusion drive here, mid-implosion. To the right and below, space, and stars.

"That's the way I would come," Flint said, pointing left to the cryosection. His voice sounded flat and dulled in this strange suspension.

"It touches several parts of the ship," Jack said. It hadn't always, though. Most likely the glamour demon grew the fracture.

"How are we floating?" Flint asked.

"Space fractures are also time fractures. Your gun may not shoot here," Jack said.

Your paint won't fly here either, will it?

"It won't," Jack said.

She looked at her flame, now static. Little flakes of paint peeled away and rose, higher and higher in an upward stream. Jack's glove next, then her very hand.

Jack might have panicked if she didn't recognise the peeling streams for what they were. Glamour. Still, Jack felt for her goggles with her free hand.

"Wait!" Flint said. The top of his head appeared to

disintegrate in vertical shafts. Light came from all the realities, green from the cryosection. Yellow from the vacuum of space, and broken sunlight from the falling hub behind them. It danced through the particles he appeared to become.

"It's not real," Jack said. "Keep your wits." Not a bad glamour in a reality shard. She pulled her goggles off and tucked the strap into her belt.

Wolfgang, too, appeared to come apart in bars of arachnid armour, hair, and tender flesh, streamers flying up from her as they did from Flint and Jack. The space looked like a forest of lines above them as they disintegrated. Wolfgang sheathed her sword and drew her jade ward brush.

In the part of the fracture that showed stars, the void of space writhed. Ripples like gravitational lensing emanated, except these were organic. Even Jack felt her gorge rise, as the ripples evoked worms behind the fabric of reality.

Yet Jack had seen behind the fabric of reality, and it was worse to behold than this. Either this was the demon herself, settled into a physical form, or a glamour distraction.

Time appeared to change in the space part of the fracture. The view of the cosmos sped up, and a small part of Jack felt fear, watching stars die in supernovas, time cooling, and in the flitting motion of the cosmos. For who could behold eternity and not gasp?

Flint screamed.

"Hold," Jack said. For a pattern emerged in the changing space: a nebula, and then a black hole, but always an eye. First a galactic disk, then a superstructure of dyson spheres, but always a mouth, and the teeth in that mouth moved of their own accord like living solar flares.

Jack felt her bandoliers tugged, now covered in upward streamers of their own in the illusion. The demon thought to rob her? Well, fair was fair, she supposed, even if the

Sixteen Canvas was made for painter knights and only painter knights.

Jack remembered her hand holding the flame ball. Despite its changed appearance, it was still there in her hand. Jack released the ball and pushed the flame away. Sparks flew nearby where it met some panel or metal. With that hand, she touched reality where the demon's thieving arm hid behind the streamers. Jack felt liquid there, a half-formed solid.

Next would be difficult. Reality had a fabric, and it had colour, a pigment. Scientists in history had called these gluons or quarks or some such, but paintslingers manipulated these, and called them pigment. So Jack focused on the pigment. And when she pulled her hand away, she brought the colour of reality away from its fabric.

True black there, the space behind the world stuff, and behind that, malevolence. The illusion of disintegrating ceased, for on Jack's fingers, the colour of the real dripped.

With the illusion gone, sharded reality still bent light. In the space section of the shard, the demon face in the cosmos screamed. The stars wavered making the face appear childlike, yet huge. The neck came into being and the arms, slick things. It screamed, then vanished.

Streamers stopped coming off Flint and Wolfgang. Flint touched himself, examined his fingers. Wolfgang warded herself and Flint, though Jack was too far away. They were whole, but the fracture still bent corners, turned the eye uncomfortably, and let them view the joins of space and time where reality flickered around them. Among the flickering, the corners showed the ship again, cryosection, centrifuge, and space, all meeting in this impossible junction.

"To the cryosection," Jack said. For when the demon died, they'd do better than resuming their fall in the collapsing centrifuge.

Wolfgang gripped Flint and pushed off against the floating debris.

Jack tried to do the same, but didn't move. She tried harder.

A huge force pulled at her paint bandolier and—

A blur of air and force. Jack felt her chin hit her chest hard. Her arms flew out in front of her. On instinct, she tried and failed to reach for her brush and goggles.

Pain. Vision faded with impact against the frozen collapsing centrifuge. Breath refused to come into Jack's lungs at first, then she inhaled sharply.

The goggles? They weren't on her head.

Jack looked at her hands. She appeared to have six fingers apiece, then four. More glamour, more dissembling. And possibly a lost pair of goggles after being thrown by a giant glamour demon.

She couldn't draw her brush, yet. Soon, though.

The demon slammed into the wall next to her there and pulled at Jack's arm. Jack yanked, and a snap sounded fleshy inside her forearm.

Light pulsed behind Jack's eyes as the alarms of pain shot through her whole arm.

Pain was not suffering. Pain was not suffering. Pain...well it was certainly something. But the chant helped.

And the demon was losing its temper now. Jack was closer to the cryosection.

Jack angled her body, implying escape, and if she did it right, the demon would throw her this way and...

Another force.

Jack's ears rang with the impact.

She opened her eyes and found herself on the ceiling. Because of course. Upside down again. Jack had made it into the cryosection.

The demon flickered into being and loomed over her, a

PAINTSLINGER

hole in its tail where Jack had pulled the pigment out of it. It didn't bleed, as Jack didn't put any blood there. It just lost a part of itself. Which apparently made it somewhat angry.

It swung an arm at her, its shape changing as it moved through the folds of the real and became just an avatar arm.

Jack was out of the fracture. The ship was a ship again. She stood instead of drifting in the void between realities. The demon was before her, just a huge, incomplete avatar, mad and powerless without her glamours.

Brush out, and Jack had the pigment of the thing on her fingers still, didn't she? She got the paint on the brush and let it fly. The demon's hand became a stump.

Jack stood up on the cryosection's jointed ceiling, spat something that probably wasn't spit, and spoke. "Cry mercy, and you shall have it." The words surprised Jack as they escaped. The old forms, here? Perhaps it was the canvas. Still, the forms had been voiced, and Jack was glad to have spoken them.

Wolfgang visibly paused. She had noticed, too.

The demon clutched at its own chest. Jack saw the canvas there, buried under the demon's skin. The canvas could change, become shards of varied size, and it glowed behind the demon's avatar flesh.

The demon pulled the shards out with its working hand, exposing bio and electrical matter, and launched itself upward for a cryotube of larger size.

Jack dipped the brush in iron-white and let fly a missile, sharp as any blade at this close range. It sliced the demon's finger on that hand and the canvas's shard flew free, then hovered out of the demon's reach.

The canvas was there, free of the demon, ready to be taken, expanded, used to create and destroy worlds.

These were her thoughts. So when words escaped, they surprised even Jack.

"Cry pardon," Jack offered again, "and you shall have it."

Flint moved.

He drew, quick as ever. His finger on the trigger, that click of cylinder action and hammer cocking. Jack's hands moved as they knew to move, throwing verte green paint out at speed. The cylinder clicked, the hammer fell, and the bullet exploded out. Paint met the bullet in air and exploded in a cloud of verdant light. The smell of fresh grass and living forest filled the dry old ship.

Flint looked at Jack.

"Hold," Jack said. "Last chance, demon. Would you have our mercy?"

The demon turned and made again for the cryotube.

"We have to stop it," Flint said.

"Hold," Jack said. "It might be fleeing, and we might be letting it. The canvas is there, floating." The finger-sized shard of flat crystal rotated, shining in the lingering green cloud.

The cryotube began to close, the door hissing, and glowed bright blue. The cycling of the ship's air resumed. The demon was becoming the ship again.

I share your views of mercy, but letting the demon escape is unwise, no?

Jack limped forward and took hold of the canvas chard. It collapsed itself more slowly than she remembered, folding smaller and flatter, but how long had it been? The canvas became an elongated flat diamond shape on her palm, smooth and impossibly black.

The cycling pushed air in, then out.

In, out, in and out again.

Jack. Do we run? The demon is there in the tube.

No need to run. Not with the canvas. Besides, they were too far in the ship to flee. It had taken them all night to get here.

PAINTSLINGER

The air cycled harder, harder still, and became a torrent, dust flying and scraping against skin and cloth alike. Jack tried to use her broken arm to raise her bandanna but pain settled that score and she had to use the hand holding the canvas. Mask on and goggles—

Ah, she had put them on her belt, and there they still hung.

Before she could don them, the other avatars swarmed in by the light of the huge cryotube. Flint shadowed his face with one hand and raised the gun with the other. But the avatars weren't coming for them.

"Hold!" Jack said.

The avatars jumped on the cryotube, pulling it apart, with sparks flying and fire billowing out in the cryosection. Under the swarm, the glamour demon fought and screamed, but it was exposed, not yet part of the ship, and the avatars finished their work quickly.

Mob justice was ugly, but Jack was no judge here. How many of these avatars had she and her friends just destroyed.

A hum built as the avatars dispersed. The ship didn't breathe any more, just ventilated, as old automated systems resumed. Gravity stayed upside down, though. The demon must have used a ship system for that, so the automations didn't set it aright.

And who should come out of the fray when the avatars made their work of the demon but the avatar with the painted metal plate on the scalp.

"Hello, friend," Jack said. "You got some help?"

The avatar pointed to the back of one of the others, which wore makeshift metal plates, scraps that covered enough of the spot to allow thought, free of the demon's control. Yet those wouldn't have been enough at first. A song had freed the first of these, Jack was sure. But that would mean that this unspeaking avatar knew the song magic and used it.

"I thank you for your help. Flint, Wolfgang, will you check this isn't some glamour trick?"

They did as she asked. The avatar pointed to Jack's broken arm.

"You can splint this?"

The avatar nodded.

"I'll ask you for that shortly," Jack said. "First I need to make a door."

She held out the canvas and watched it float off her skin at eye level and unfold into a fractal. She waited for the next unfolding. She waited some more. And more. Jack walked closer to the blue light of the shattered cryotube and the dying flames, examining the canvas.

By the light of fire, she could just see it for what it was.

Instead of being forever smooth as it should have been, cut lines criss-crossed the surface of the obsidian shapes.

The canvas was fake.

−•−

The next day, Jack stood on the rocky scree outside the ship and examined her splint in the evening light. Without the canvas, they'd had to climb back through the wreckage of the ship.

"This is a good splint, avatar. Do you speak?"

The avatar nodded and became purely female and opened her mouth, closed it, and opened it again.

"That's alright," said Jack. "I suppose it's been a long time."

She nodded but pressed on, working her jaw.

A melodic voice said, "Ro-Sa-Hu." Definitely the voice of the singer she'd heard in the centrifuge. Yet it still sounded familiar from before this ship and this time.

Jack realised Rosahu was watching her. "Rosahu. A good

name. I thank you for your aid, Rosahu. Your fellows didn't take kindly to the first part of our encounter, but you forgave our encroachment." Jack paused. This avatar had used song magic to rescue her ship mates, then mimicked Jack's paint with real metal to free them. No small feat, regardless of the old question.

Jack added, "I hope to work with you again if your power allows you to leave. Give Wolfgang a way to contact you and keep something covering that spot." Jack tapped the top of her head with her good hand.

The ship will be waiting for us, Wolfgang said.

The ship that Jack shouldn't have needed; yes, she hadn't forgot.

Flint stepped forward. "I'm sorry about your canvas. We sure appreciate you helping us."

"You are kind. Likewise, should you care to venture beyond this place, I could use a gun hand."

He looked down and kicked a small stone, and Jack could see him trying to prepare some response.

"Of course, your village may need you more," Jack said.

"I think they might." Flint said.

Jack inclined her head and hefted her pack with easel and mixing tent with her unbroken arm, then pulled her goggles and mask into place. She and Wolfgang headed for the space port, empty-handed.

CHAPTER SEVEN

Wylan Ronde returned to the dragon court.

She could almost believe the dummy on the throne was a man. Giant thorns grew up around the gilded chair such that, to the casual observer, the throne, dais, and wall might just seem to be ornate finery. And was it her imagination, or did the man-doll seem more fleshy than usual? Did the painted eyes there move and follow her?

Wylan approached the dais and knelt.

The forever voice of the dragon almost sounded small enough to come from the man-doll.

"Done?" the dragon asked.

"The canvas is disposed of as you commanded, my Emperor, and replaced with a forgery of my own considerable skill," Wylan said.

"Not destroyed?"

"My Emperor, to do so would cause imbalance." Also, the anger of a dragon. "I neither create nor destroy. Etcetera. I rest with my emperor, seeking enlightenment."

"An old lie," the dragon said. "But you help me, and that will do. Out of interest, where is the canvas now?"

"Beyond the bardo worlds where your magic aids inhabitants."

The man-doll actually moved its head down and looked at

Wylan. Well, well. The dragon really was becoming human. Wonders never ceased.

"Next I would—" the dragon began.

"Yes, my Emperor?"

"Next—"

The doll slumped, a stringless puppet once more. The thorns glimmered, no longer the twisted branches of a tornado-torn forest or a mountainside after an eruption. The huge wall became dragon horns once more, a mass of them that comprised the periphery of its buried head below the dais.

The floor shook. Marble cracked and the gilded pillars flaked gold.

"I'll just excuse myself," Wylan stayed bowed and backed from the room.

"Magic." The dragon voice boomed from everywhere.

Wylan paused, still bowed, at the great arches.

"Someone creates. A painter," the dragon said. The steam billowed out below the dais. The dummy's arms and legs flopped in the force of the dragon breath. "Find them."

Not exactly Wylan's idea of being a Court Bard. Not really part of the deal, you might say. It was all about the lute and the cushion. Then again, this magic must be pretty strong to extend the dragon's life. Maybe a challenge to break up all this enlightenment business could help pass the time.

"I shall help the painter escape samsara," Wylan said.

The red of the dais rug caught fire. Wylan excused herself.

She had a painter to kill.

—•—

On a port planet far from the world with the generation ship, the paintslinger walked through a daylit forest. Back in the space port, beggars had accosted her as a traveller, then been surprised when she joined them. She sketched the traders and travellers in exchange for food and supplies. She'd also sketched Wolfgang, Flint, Rosahu, and other companions, like Uma Kozak, the equine maker of legend in her horse armour. No travellers recognised these, but they accepted the sketches happily, and if Jack was a little slow to hand them over, they didn't notice.

With travel supplies gathered, her arm sore but healing with nanodrink help, Jack ventured into the forest. First she walked on paths, then when those ended, she stepped over brush and under branch. When the sounds of people faded, she walked for another two hours. Part of her wondered at her own temperament, missing the past, and yet escaping those as would have her company in the present. Though, she had to be careful. If she thought too far back, she could touch dangerous memories—those she'd rather not harm by revisiting.

Jack focused on her breathing and walked on. At long last, she came to a peepal tree in a clearing and unlimbered. Its semicircular canopy and gnarled trunk offered shelter and a place to rest. Jack settled her pack and sat. The babble of water nearby made for a nice replacement from the bustle she'd left behind. Good place for her mixing tent.

A heart-shaped leaf fell on her crossed legs, and she left it there. She drank from her water flask. Another leaf fell. A third.

Jack settled her brush bag across her legs and continued hydrating.

A biped canine in beggar's robes stepped into the clearing. "Kind words to you!" she said.

She set down her mortal and pestle, trying not to sigh aloud. Sure, canines were respected throughout the worlds for their role in lifting many species to sentience, but Jack did not know this person, and she needed to mix her paints.

However, these customs should not be ignored.

In an age before, canines had worked with paintslinger knights, creating world hubs that brought security to civilisations across universes. The Lifters had earned their honoured place.

Perhaps mixing and meditation could wait long enough to appease this weary traveller and point her in the right direction.

"Hail, Auntie," Jack said, keeping custom when addressing an elder and a canine. "There's a stream further on. I wish you safety on your path."

"Oh, I'll just settle here a moment," the canine said. "I look forward to the company of an artist. Tell me, did I see correctly that some of your drawings were very good?"

Some? Jack began packing her things. "You're too kind to a poor artist such as I."

"Maybe," the canine said. She sat beside Jack and crossed her legs. "Why, some of the drawings even seemed to come to life under your skilful hand."

"Beg pardon, Auntie, but I don't know what you mean."

"Oh, you just reminded me of tales from my home world. It was the paintslingers that aided the canines against the marauders after our world hub was built, you know."

"Mmm," Jack said. If she stopped talking the canine might leave.

"Yes. And you know, rumours say there was a paintslinger that saved a planet from a demon not two months ago? What are the odds of that. A paintslinger after all these years."

Jack closed her eyes and pretended to nod off.

"Oh, but I do go on," the canine said. "Say, wake up now! Would you draw a poor beggar such as myself? It calms my energy to see such talent. Use this brush." She reached a dexterous paw toward the thin satchel in Jack's lap.

Jack pulled the satchel away and drew a brush from her hip without thinking.

The canine looked from her drawn brush to her satchel and back, then smiled.

Just breathe, Jack. Keep breathing.

She placed the brush back in the bag and pulled the bag closer to her. "Beg pardon, Auntie, but your kind paws should not dirty themselves on such as my brushes."

The canine smiled more and closed her eyes in apparent bliss.

"You hold the brush just like them, you know, like a weapon. And in their hands, it truly is a weapon. I believe I'll follow you for a while. Never mind the drawing."

"You mistake me," Jack lied.

"You may call me Shen Fang," the canine said.

Not names. Wolfgang wasn't due for days and the food she'd begged for would go very thin with an elder guest. "An honour," Jack said.

"And you? What do they call you?" The eyes-closed smile again.

"Jack."

"Oh, exotic, I like it."

"Thank you, Auntie."

Shen Fang smiled. "What are we eating?"

"Grain and broth, if it suits you."

They shared a bowl and the grain Jack had traded and begged for. Shen Fang ate two meals worth and gave twice that in prying banter, before declaring, "It's late! I think I'll sleep here by your fire. You should rest as well. Go on. Lie back. You will not need a tent on a clear night such as this. Sleep well!"

PAINTSLINGER

Shen Fang slept within seconds, leaving Jack to clean up.

After, Jack laid back and slept in the way of the travellers: deep enough to dream, but not so deep they couldn't wake should someone try to rob them. Before first light, Jack rose and packed her few belongings. Shen Fang snored all through the ritual.

One night of palaver and done. Customs had been maintained. Safe travels and fare thee well, Auntie.

Once clear of the snoozing canine, Jack hurried on and spent the morning walking further into the forest. Hours later, though, when Jack came to another clearing, Shen Fang looked up.

"Hello friend! Good idea hunting separately this morning. What did you catch?"

Jack did not frown, and made every effort to not do so.

And so the next several days went. Jack ate little and slept less until Wolfgang arrived.

Which, of course, happened in the rain. At night. With Shen Fang in Jack's tent.

Jack heard Wolfgang approaching and stepped out to meet her, shielding herself from the dripping water from the canopy above.

Good to see you, Jackson, Wolfgang said in writing.

"Hail, Wolfgang. You found me alright?" Jack asked.

I almost didn't. Your trail looked unusual. You aren't alone?

"It's a story I don't care to tell right now, though I think she's harmless."

If you insist. Regardless, I come with new work for us. Exciting work.

"You only say that when you think it's bad. It's not a world with money is it?"

No, of course not. It involves of travel. You enjoy the travel, yes?

"A world hub palaver, then? You should know better, friend. The canine art is lost and even if it wasn't, the creation of a world hub would start a war across realities."

Yes, as before. A war which would require a Sixteen Court to end.

"Never mind. Let's rest for the time being, perhaps on a different planet. We'll get passage on some ship. You can write and I can sketch."

Wolfgang moved her head up and down in such a way that Jack knew was amused. It was her arachnid equivalent of smiling.

This task offers payment in advance.

"You said it wasn't a money world?"

It isn't. Our patron, Shen Fang...

But Jack missed the rest of the floating words. She pulled back the tent flap. Shen Fang drank soup from the bowl and waved, blissful in the light of Jack's lamp. In Jack's tent. With Jack's bowl.

After slurping, Shen Fang spoke. "Kind words to you, Wolfgang! It's good to see you again."

Kind words to you, Lifter. I see you've already met Jack.

"Yes, she's very gracious you know. Now, about that task I have for the two of you." Shen Fang stood and stepped into the rainy night. Three moons lit the forest behind those clouds and the light reflected off Shen Fang's wetting fur. So, Shen Fang had known all along?

"What would you have us do?" Jack asked.

"We have a world hub," Shen Fang said. "It's almost complete. But the neighbouring realities are dangerous. We'll need someone to travel and secure them."

Easy to refuse, because regardless of the payment, Jack's forever paint was not going to last forever, and she had no canvas to travel the worlds. Without a canvas, until the world hub was complete, if indeed it ever was without destroying that part of its universe, travel was by bardo worlds, by ships between planets, or by thin places, and she'd rather not travel by thin place. Horrors shared across realities made poor corridors. Even if all of those facts weren't true, it was futile to consider. The Sixteen Court was gone, and the secret must be kept.

A picture flashed in Jack's mind of the grand entrance to the Sixteen Court, arch gates with flowing paint like a living, moving Van Gogh image, and Jack pressed the image down. Memories change in the remembering.

"I'm afraid we can't help you," Jack said.

"Payment in advance," Shen Fang said. "Well, sort of. A loan, maybe. Until the task is complete. Then it's yours."

"What would you have that I want to borrow?" Jack asked.

"Why, a Sixteen Canvas, of course!"

Jack stood silent in the rain for what seemed a long time. It must be a lie, though the Lifters were not known to dissemble, at least not directly. They spoke of truth as having layers. More likely this was an error. Another clever forgery.

"There isn't paint," Jack said finally. "The gift demon lied. And the last of the Eldritch died. I can't get tears from the Elders, so there's no more forever paint."

That's not entirely true, Wolfgang said. *There is a way.*

"You say true," Jack said. "If we went back in time to the same dying Old One, we could cross ourselves."

But you remember crossing a future self, there, no?

"Am I that future self, brushmaster? What if I go back now and need to go back again later?"

You would need a canvas to go back, which suddenly you have access to.

"More than that, I'd need help. I couldn't travel back to aid the Eldritch alone. Kozak could help us, but supposedly she's about to be executed. She'll have an escape plan, and she won't like our barging in on it. Plus, we'd need more than her help, too."

So we rescue Kozak. And we find more help. That avatar seemed keen to follow before you left in one of your moods. Then we each get a single teardrop from the Eldritch. Yours becomes unlimited paint base. And then we accept the task, no?

Shen Fang watched the exchange. She pulled a sketch from the folds of her robe. The sentient horse, Uma Kozak with three metal prosthetic arms, worked at one of her maker desks. Shen Fang must have traded for the sketch after Jack completed it.

Well. It would seem Jack was out of excuses, and Shen Fang had known it all along. Jack wanted to see the canvas for herself. The shard was almost definitely a fake, perhaps constructed alongside the counterfeit on Flint's world. But imagining it wasn't, Jack fought rising hope. "Where is the canvas?" Jack asked.

"The canvas shard is in a safe place in the city," Shen Fang said. She pointed in the direction of the space port. "The equine comes first."

There was something different about this Lifter.

"We can attempt to gather Kozak," Jack said, "but with no guarantees. If we interrupt her escape plan, she won't be amenable. And the equine civilisation is not kind to criminals or those who would interfere with their interpretation of justice."

"Wonderful," Shen Fang said, apparently ignoring Jack's warnings. "Let's finish dinner and go in the morning. Unless someone is willing to pack us up now."

"As you say, Auntie. I'll break camp now." The sooner she examined the supposed canvas, the better.

"Oh good," Shen Fang said. "I'll just eat the rest while you pack."

Shen Fang stepped into the tent.

She's amicable.

"Considerably," Jack said.

Jack broke camp and, stomach growling, made for town with the arachnid and the canine.

CHAPTER EIGHT

At night under aurora lights, a sentient horse stepped onto a raised platform. The local Justice of the Equine People prepared to address the horse citizens around the galaxy by teleportal. The Justice hated teleportals. The glowing oval rings as tall as a horse floated around the Justice, showing views to equine crowds watching and waiting. She shifted under the ceremonial robotic headdress and armour. Thank the horse gods she only had to wear it on these rare occasions. The night wind howled under the aurora, so much so that words would have to be shouted.

The condemned horse, Uma Kozak, stood proud, despite being stripped of both armour and robotic limbs. Judging by the hubris on her face and in her eyes, Kozak might do just that.

If Kozak disseminated, uncomfortable truths might surface, and it would be the Justice facing these watching portals, rather than the criminal. It would be the Justice stripped of armour and prostheses and sent through an ancient gate into the collapsing galaxy, condemned to the mercy or judgement of samsara.

Kozak stamped her hoof. The impatient horse wasted her last few moments.

Kozak deserved this result. It did not matter that her crime

PAINTSLINGER

had saved lives. Nor did it matter who orchestrated the actions requiring the crime in the first place. The public need not know that, and laws must be kept.

The portals hung as rings of energy around the platform. Each showed masses of gathered citizens. Except one. One portal flickered. Sputtered. Changed. Which was impossible. The teleportals were a passive medium. Only the execution gate, not yet summoned, would allow travel, and that travel one way to a dying galaxy.

Arachnid wards circled the outside of that teleportal, and the view replaced itself.

The Justice looked to Kozak. Was she behind this? No, she looked angry at the change. She seemed to be cursing into the wind.

Instead of masses of equine citizens, this portal showed a homosapien in goggles and dusty old clothes, an arachnid in non-sapient armour, a tel-fem with a metal plate on her head, and a canine in monk's robes.

"Do you know how to condemn someone or not?" Kozak shouted. "Give me the armour. I'll do it. Seriously. The gate is really easy to operate if you know how."

The changed portal drifted toward the platform. Were they going to come through? The teleportals shouldn't allow that, but they shouldn't drift, either.

Chaos erupted in the other portals. Mayhem among the citizens. A justice ceremony hadn't been interrupted in decades.

The Justice telepathically activated the headdress and armour. The prosthetic arms extending from her neck began the ritual that opened the gate to the collapsing galaxy.

"Come on, hurry," Kozak said, which was odd, but there wasn't time to inspect Kozak's reactions.

The misbehaving portal floated alongside the platform.

The four trespassers stepped out beside the Justice. The homosapien female gestured.

The tel-fem nodded and grew herself until she was eye to eye with the Justice, tendons stretching and popping under her skin, switching from tel-fem to tel-man and back, face expressing apprehension. And it offered some trinket to the local Justice's idle third prosthetic hand. The Justice's two main arms continued the ritual, but the third hand accepted the object and raised it up for examination.

An evidence log?

"Hey, Justice! Focus, okay?" Kozak said over the din. "It's not difficult. Just finish the ritual and open the gate. The big rectangle behind us? It connects to a supernova in progress but only if you do the ritual."

This was all confusing. Why did Kozak want the execution to progress? This was madness.

Without her consent, the Justice's third hand pressed the translucent bar to a data plate on the armour. Images flooded the Justice's mind. Because it came through the artificially intelligent armour, the scene was also broadcast to all of the High Seats.

No, no, no! She would be ruined.

Shameful truths were shown.

The Justice herself ordered Kozak to embark on the illegal mission. In the Hall of Justice itself!

"What are you doing, Jack?" Kozak shouted above the wind.

"Hail, maker!"

The colour of the teleportals rings changed from amber to cyan. The Justice stopped the ritual and stepped backward. Impossible. The decision was reversed?

"I cry your pardon," the homosapien said, patting the Justice's armour. "She is free to go, yes?"

PAINTSLINGER

The citizens of the galaxy watched. No doubt the evidence, verified by every process imaginable, would be playing out locally. They would have seen truth.

Almost, the Justice refused. But if she did, she might receive worse than Kozak was condemned to now. To do so would be refuting law that everyone watching accepted as just. So instead, the Justice shifted under the ceremonial armour and headdress, examined her prosthesis, and nodded.

"Uma Kozak, you are hereby acquitted of all wrongdoing, having been ordered by a member of government to act as you did."

"You shouldn't have come, Jack" Kozak said to the homosapien.

"You always say that," Jack said.

They stepped back into the malfunctioning teleportal. The canine beamed and waved. The arachnid saluted. The tel-fem shrunk back to the scale of the others and loped along behind.

The portal reverted to showing an equine crowd on a distant planet.

The local Justice cleared her throat and prepared to address them before charges could be made against her.

-•-

Jack led them to the galley of the cargo ship they'd bartered for passage on and prepared for Kozak's frustrations to be voiced. Fair frustrations, no doubt, but Jack wasn't looking forward to the discussion.

Kozak ducked beneath metal gangways and ducts. "Who arranged travel on this rust-bucket?"

"Nicer ships don't allow passage by barter," Jack said. "Not for sketches and drawings of the crew, anyway."

"And they do for crew on ships like this?" Kozak asked.

"No. But I can depict other things such as they find pleasing."

"Gross."

"Sometimes," Jack said.

In the halogen light of the galley, Jack sat at one of the tables and gestured for the others to do the same. The stainless steel tables were clean, but free of ornament.

"No equine mats?" Kozak said. "And who's the lucky one to feed me without my prostheses?"

Good, sarcasm was good with Kozak. It usually meant she was interested.

"We aren't here to eat," Jack said. She started to mention that the prostheses were here, but Kozak spoke first.

"You need me to help you steal something or help you lie. Which is it?" Kozak said.

"A bit of both?" Jack said.

Shen Fang added: "You shouldn't lie, you know!"

"Yes Auntie," Jack said. When no one spoke after, Jack took the opportunity. "Kozak, this is Shen Fang. She has acquired our services."

"Respect to you, Lifter," Kozak said.

Shen Fang nodded.

Hello to you, Uma. Kind words, Wolfgang said.

"Long time," Kozak said. "Still waving your forelimb around rather than getting a proper prosthetic voice, I see."

You sound like Jack offering to paint me a talking mask, Wolfgang said.

"And who's the tel-man? Or tel-fem, it seems?" Kozak asked.

"Rosahu is a ship avatar from a planet we visited," Jack said. "She's been helping us with what arises. A certain record that would pass all your government's AI checks and balances, for example. I've never depicted in code before."

"Not bad. Though anyone familiar with your handiwork

would have spotted some common mistakes. You never get my mane right," Kozak said. "So be honest. You must be pretty stuck to come rescuing me. What do you want from me this time? More nanodrinks? I do make the best."

"We have to travel using a canvas," Jack said. This time nanodrinks had nothing to do with it. Or very little.

Kozak stamped and circled. "Are you kidding me? You went through all that trouble because you thought I could help you get a Sixteen Canvas? Wow, you've gotten crazier over the years. They don't exist! Give up, Jack."

Kozak had echoed Jack's own disbelief, but Shen Fang stepped forward and unfolded a fine velvet. A crystal shard lay in its centre.

Jack reached for it.

"A loan, yes, young paintslinger?" Shen Fang said.

Jack nodded. Breathe, Jack. Just breathe.

She touched the canvas with a fingertip and it floated off the velvet, hovering before her. It would surely have the same cross-cut lines as the other ...

Impossibly smooth reflections played over the opaque crystal.

Jacked willed it and the crystal unfolded, becoming a fractal of six points, collapsing and expanding, then dividing into eight and twelve, each time shifting in shape like a geometric shoreline, simple angles yet infinite in sharp beauty.

"By the horse gods," Kozak said.

The shard hovered, floating and unfolding and evolving through fractal after fractal, random perfection from nature into another random perfection. It was a metre high. It expanded further, gaps opening and filling in the middle, until it hung large as a thin cage of crystal, shifting between three dimensional primitive outline shapes and ready for someone to step inside it.

Jack stepped inside it and the canvas cage rippled around her and settled into a crystal rhomboid with starbursts at corners. As she held up her left hand, crystalline shards materialised above her palm, ready to be painted on. They coalesced as she wanted. If she willed them, they'd be three dimensional. Or four. Or five. As she lifted her right hand, crystals formed into finer and finer patterns, become a hovering brush with which she might paint. This brush needed no handle, for her handle was her mind, though Jack preferred to see and hold something, so the handle appeared. Besides, the lower forms would require a handle, the training forms. This brush had no distance limitation, not that had been found. If Jack used the pigment of reality and painted a star in the sky, a sun would be born where she imagined it.

"Hey hey," Kozak said. "Not bad at all. Well, go on. Do something cool."

Jack hesitated a moment, then lowered her hands. The crystals flowed away, rejoining to the main shape, and the main shape disconnected itself around her and began to fold itself into separate yet joining shards.

Somehow, the canine had actually found a Sixteen Canvas, a true one. Yet without limitless paint, what could she do? The problem seemed larger than ever.

"Jack. You're ignoring me. Why didn't you paint some big creature or a portal? Unless you can't for some reason. Don't tell me: you're out of paint? You're out of paint."

"Almost out of paint," Jack said. "Enough for limited trips with the canvas."

Jack believes the gift demon lied, Wolfgang said. *A lie that even affects my wards, somehow, though not as drastically.*

"Wait, so you're thinking of going back to the Eldritch? No way. Impossible. We already did that, already made the

Eldritch weep and harvested teardrops. I got my gift, you got yours, everyone else got theirs, and we all moved on. The Eldritch is dead. Find yourself another gift demon because there are no more Old Ones, Jack. You of all people should know that."

"You aren't wrong," Jack said. "There are no more Old Ones. Our only option would be to go back in time. We'd need powerful machinations for such a task."

Kozak's nostrils flared. She no doubt recognised Jack's flattery, but that didn't mean it wasn't working. Recognition did not equal immunity.

"I'd have to depict with perfect accuracy," Jack said. "Not just space, but time and the way that the universe has changed. I'd have to know exactly where in the universe we are now, where we were then, and depict that place with an accuracy only the best that spark and spell could give me. The most realistic depiction of the past ever created."

"You really are insane," Kozak said. But she nodded in a way that usually meant: *go on.*

"That would merely be travelling there," Jack said. "We'd still have to lie to the Eldritch. Remind them of their loss. Guide them into samsara."

"If you failed, you could make us all go mad. Make us remember multiple histories. Hell, if it went very wrong you could make entire cultures change."

"You're right, of course," Jack said, trying to sound abashed. "We'd need more than just myself and those here. An entire team of makers would be required. And they'd all be rewarded. Forgive me for the underestimation of the task." A lie. Jack knew very well that Kozak was capable.

Kozak caught the implication. "How do you get me into these things?"

"Does that mean you'll help?" Jack asked.

"You said you have enough paint to make a few trips?" Kozak asked.

Jack nodded, and if she let herself smile a little, so much the better. A real canvas here, and a team, and Jack couldn't think of a better turn of events.

"Don't start grinning yet. Get me my prosthetic arms, and I'm in."

"I anticipated this request. They're in your quarters. I tried to tell you earlier," Jack said.

"Ass," Kozak said.

"Fair," Jack said.

"Well I'm going to put my arms on. See you crazy people in the morning," Kozak said.

Uma Kozak, aren't you glad to have been rescued?

"You think I needed rescuing? I arranged a sentient ship on the other side of the gate before I even broke the law just in case. She'll leave without me, don't worry. Good night."

She left the galley and the others followed, all but Wolfgang.

Do you think we can make the Eldritch weep with our past selves there? Wolfgang asked.

"We can try," Jack said.

We can try, Wolfgang agreed.

CHAPTER NINE

Two more cargo ships and a mindship journey later, Jack and the others arrived at one of her abodes. Jack stood on the scraggy hill in the morning light of a standard gravity, one g, one sun planet and gestured to the manor estate down the path. Cold air of winter rushed into her duster.

Ahead, a brick wall with ironwork circled a large maintained park with paths, bare trees, and wildlife. In the centre of the park, a manor house stood with brick facade, pillars with capitals, and tall stained glass windows. From this height, the U-shape symmetry of the manor house was visible, three storeys tall with a large entrance hall in the centre and wings at both sides. Good construction, if Jack did say so herself. Even old creations had a kind of merit.

Rosahu stood beside Jack. She shrank to Jack's size and tried to speak. "You st ... st-stay here?"

"It's not hers," Kozak said. Was Kozak more rude now that she had her armour and prosthesis? "Bet me. Anyone. Wolfgang?"

Wolfgang looked to Shen Fang as if considering whether to take the bet while the canine listened.

"Hold your supplies, Wolfgang," Jack said. "You'd lose. Folks on this planet don't own places. The previous occupants abandoned it, digitised themselves and began living in a mindship's simulation." Just because Jack had painted this manor into existence didn't make it hers. It was a commune where artists could rest, read, and paint when they needed.

Winding down through the yellowed grass of winter, the wear and gravel of a thousand years marked the path. Granite stairs let up the outside of the wall, wide and flat enough for Kozak to climb with no problems, and once inside the wall, they navigated the paths and walkways to the interior.

Shen Fang paused. She knelt and pried at a crack in the granite. A pebble came free and the crack disappeared.

"Magic?" Shen Fang asked.

"Or nanorepair?" Kozak asked.

Jack shrugged. "A traveller who stayed here before tried to find out. He kept breaking a wall in one of the sitting rooms and recording it healing itself. I wasn't here, but it wasn't wise."

"What did he find?" Kozak asked.

"I don't think the walls took kindly to his constant damage. He vanished. Nothing could be done."

Kozak considered that for a moment. "Let's call it magic," she said. Though Jack heard in her voice, she thought otherwise.

Around a fountain to the huge double door that marked the entrance of the manor, Jack paused. A series of clicks sounded behind the wood, and the doors opened of their own accord. Jack led them into the entrance hall.

Inside, marble tiles of alternating ivory and ebony receded from them to a great oak stairway with landings at intervals. To the left and right, open doorways led to other chambers. Jack breathed in the slight must of the place, paint and plaster, gold-leaf and dust in tapestry and rug, overlaying the woodsmoke draft cutting through the outside air. And if part of her examined the curved ceiling and the art lining the walls, checking for other damages from visitors, Jack could perhaps be forgiven.

"Explore, make quarters inside or out, and let's gather in the great hall, that way, in two hours." Jack pointed to her left beyond a statue. Two hours should allow each to groom, rest, or feed as their culture permitted.

I shall take first watch, Wolfgang said.

"If you like," Jack said, "but this place will protect itself and anyone in it from every kind of malice. I pity those who mean harm trying to walk that path."

Rosahu shivered at that. She grew muscles on her frame.

As the others explored, going up the ornate stair or along the manor's many chambers, Rosahu seemed torn. This place must be very different after so long in the ruins of the ship.

"You may remain with me if you like," Jack said after the others drifted on ahead.

Rosahu nodded.

"Assist me with tinder and coal?" Jack asked. "If we circle the courtyard and arcade arches, there are covered racks with plenty."

Rosahu cocked her head to the side. She seemed worried. Perhaps she knew of the thinking trees on other worlds?

"No sentient trees here," Jack added.

Rosahu nodded and joined Jack.

They carried armloads and sacks, their steps echoing on marble, and Jack appreciated the quiet noises of simple labour. Once they gathered enough wood and coal to last for hours, Jack walked back to the front door, dusted off, and carried her supplies into the great hall.

The room, longer than it was wide, stretched high above Jack's head. The marble floor contained rugs and ottomans, and a wooden bench running the length of the window wall. Light from the high windows spilled onto the oak panelling and blackened iron hearth, and motes drifted all the way to the chandeliers and curved ornate ceiling above.

On every spare inch of wall or ceiling, paintings hung with cracked gold leaf frames.

"Your paintings?" Rosahu asked.

"I didn't paint them, if that's what you mean." No, she'd painted the walls that held them. Still, this was Jack's selection.

Dali, de Chiricho, Francis Bacon, the shared minds of Tau Beta five, the collaboration of Freemantle and Stutzman, and so many others hung in the bars of winter light.

Rosahu pointed to an abstract expressionist piece near the corner of the room. Bone white splashes and daisy yellow flecks of paint criss-crossed the canvas. Foreground of these, vertical spills formed blue poles rising askew.

"Does it please you?" Jack asked.

Rosahu said nothing. Fair enough. Abstract expressionism had met many doubters. But it needed to be seen properly before judging.

Jack withdrew a brush to light the fire and the chandeliers. Then she remembered her new predicament and put the brush away once more. She struck the hearth flame with tinder and flint. Winter was perhaps the only thing to make it past the manor's defences, and the fire was slow in catching.

Rosahu pointed to the flame. "Will the castle defend this?" she asked.

"The hearth is meant for flame. The home might feel differently if we built this fire against the far wall," Jack said.

As the flames licked greedily at the dry wood, Jack sat a few metres back on the crimson rug. She wasn't avoiding the chez lounges or ottomans. Furniture wasn't alive like the manor, though the home might try to keep it in repair. No, Jack preferred the rug near the fire.

Rosahu sat beside her.

"Wolfgang mentioned you had some idea of how you'd help us on our task," Jack said.

Rosahu waved her hand in a see-saw gesture. Not sure.

"You know the Eldritch imparts gifts if it dies," Jack said. "Everyone who aids the telling receives their own teardrop, and for each, this gift will be unique."

The old phrase from the Court came to mind: in the world of the weeping, no shortage of tears. Jack felt a pang, and realised Rosahu shook her head.

"No? Well think about what might serve you. It will be a part of the Old One, but such gifts are known to have magic beyond our microscopes and our study."

"Could it help me s ... s-speak?"

How best to answer this? The Eldritch might just grant that request. But was Rosahu ready for what that might entail?

"Some call such things dark magic. For me, it's a dangerous path to change yourself in a moment. For what if the new you despises the old and never surrenders? What if the new you becomes something the core of you judges as false or unkind?"

Rosahu looked to the belt of vials at Jack's side and said, "Those change you."

"Indeed. Some might equate nanodrinks and change magic. I measure augmentation as different from becoming someone else entirely, though I admit it's an exercise in grey areas. When I drink these, I'm Jack with night vision or Jack with EM vision. Just as you might grow and shrink, become male or fem while you remain Rosahu."

Again, she see-sawed her hand. And she was right to do so.

"Exactly," Jack said. "What is 'Rosahu'? That's the conundrum. Rosahu is something you and I believe. You alone get to make the call on what that means. You carry all the things that comprise him or her, body and memory and mind, pleasure and pain and every mix of the two. With change magic, you can never be specific enough of what you want kept and what you don't. You may say 'make me kinder,' but what if that costs you the memories that made you hard? You may say 'make me stronger,' but what if you lose the vulnerability that makes you friend to those you love? Only when such changes are made inside you do they have a chance in samsara of taking the rest of who you are into account."

Rosahu rocked and looked into the fire.

Noises from the entrance hall echoed to them.

Jack rose, and joints popped. Maybe the furniture would be good after all.

She crossed by the hearth and met Kozak in the entrance hall. Kozak wore her linen under armour and her three prosthetic arms: two elbowed limbs and one smaller on the right. In her arms, she carried a tangle of metal equipment.

"Where did you have that?" Jack asked. "Was that in your pack?"

"None of your business. Are you going to help me or not?"

"Naturally," Jack said.

"Don't drop it. Take the flexor and the resin reservoir. No. No not that. Do you even understand my words? Stop. No never mind, I've got it."

Kozak managed to carry it into the great hall and began setting up behind the chez lounge.

"What is it all?" Jack asked.

"Complicated. This will allow me to work on what we need."

Jack held her hands up.

Wolfgang entered from the opposite way and wrote to Jack, *Uma Kozak has you surrendering already?*

"You could say she does," Jack said. "Did you see Shen

PAINTSLINGER

Fang on your way here?"

I did not. Shall I seek her?

Jack shook her head. The canine would join when she fancied.

"We need to get Rosahu up to speed on the plan," Jack said.

"You need to get us all up to speed," Kozak said. "How in all the worlds are you planning to help the same Old One as before? And don't give me flattery."

Jack nodded and looked to Rosahu. "Allow me to explain. Old Ones, or the Eldritch as some folks call them, require something of a performance as they pass from this life. Strong magic, such as all of us might bring. Spark and spell alike can lie to the dying. It will be Kozak, Wolfgang, and Rosahu with me. We'll have a Warder, a Painter, an Engineer in Kozak. And Rosahu?"

"I s ... s-sing," she said.

"As you say," Jack said. Indeed she did. But a problem Jack had been avoiding rose within her mind. In the past, Jack had not brought a singer, yet a song had been there. So this time, all the song magic would be required of Rosahu.

Shen Fang walked into the room gracefully. "And you'll have an old monk!"

Jack froze.

"Unless that's a problem, youngling?"

"Of course not, Auntie," Jack said. "Still, there are risks involved."

"Sure, sure. You'll have to take extra care of me! Besides, it would be unwholesome for me to allow the canvas away. Something could happen to you, and my people need the canvas, you understand."

So they had a patron.

"You were saying?" Kozak said. She assembled what appeared to be a work bench from the tangle of pieces. New pieces grew from the frame and filled in gaps.

"So I was," Jack said. "I was saying that there was a barrier before. A mountain of rubble erupting from some kind of portal. On the opposite side, others were there building, too. We worked together."

"Hmm," Shen Fang said. "Are you telling us there will be two parties already there as well as us?"

"No, one other party there, with us as the second party," Jack said.

"You think," Kozak said.

Jack stared at the fire and remembered the other painter's work. Such shapes she'd seen, before, forms she thought beyond her forever. And yet ... they were her strokes. Or what they might be with hundreds of years more practice. And perhaps a Sixteen Canvas.

"I'm sure," Jack said. "We were both sets of builders. Kozak did you not praise the cleverness of the spark golems for years to come?"

"Animatrons. And so what? They were done well. Not often you see well-done animatrons. They use a technique I had just developed myself, actually, where you—"

I see. She compliments someone, Wolfgang interrupted.

"So she does," Jack said.

"Well, well. You might be right," Kozak said.

Rosahu looked lost. Which was just as well, because it was time for Jack to see what she could do.

CHAPTER TEN

Jack said: "Now we're all here and washed from our travels, we need to show our friend here how we help the Old Ones. Kozak, can you build some proxy golems? Something you already have handy?"

"Animatrons. And yeah. I'll start printing them now."

"Wolfgang, the story wards only, please."

As you say, Wolfgang said.

"Now?" Rosahu asked. She seemed nervous, but the way she bounced on her toes suggested she might be excited as well.

Jack nodded. "Wolfgang told you some of what we require?"

Rosahu stood and nodded.

"Good," Jack said. "This isn't a concert, and it isn't a musical of any sort, any more than it is a painting gallery."

Shen Fang raised a paw. "Does that mean we just tell the Eldritch a story? I always enjoyed acting it out."

Jack took off her duster and tossed it aside. She pulled her goggles down to around her neck and rolled up her sleeves.

"If the Eldritch sees my paint or any other piece of this," Jack said, "we've failed. When watchers see the strings, the puppet golems die. We have to be effective enough together that the pieces disappear. That's partly down to our craft, but the Eldritch knows its dying, so even the most real paint and ward would ring false. We need older magic. Song magic."

"Change magic?" Rosahu asked.

"Of a sort," Jack said. "These Old Ones are dying. They'll expire while we're there. In an old agreement, we'll lie to them and change them. And as you know, old magic, song magic, pervades. It goes inside the listener, syncs up with them, and changes them from the inside. This can compel them to act, or tell them false is true, or even change flesh to stone."

Shen Fang leaned in. Would she point out that song magic was mostly illegal? For who knew when compulsion was voluntary? Only the low forms, projections of breath or chord to cut or burn, were allowed. Projectiles and shields, exterior song. Yet it was the compulsion magic that would convince the Eldritch to believe their lies.

Jack waited for Shen Fang to interject, but Kozak spoke first.

"In the past, we saw *BREATH OF FIRE*, too. Low forms, not just the compulsion songs."

Jack looked to Rosahu.

Rosahu paused, breathed deeply, and stepped wide and low, her knees at ninety degree angles, and raised her arms in the ancient pose that first helped breathing. She lowered her arms and exhaled sharply from pursed lips like a martial artist might breathe while striking. Raised, and lowered again, and with each pump of her arms, a push of air. After six of these, a spark drifted from her mouth. After ten, a tongue of flame flared bright in front of her. More, and the fire began to hover and remain there near her face, flickering umbers flashing light on her pale avatar face.

"Can you throw it?" Kozak asked.

Rosahu kept her stance low, but shifted around the flame so that she faced the hearth. Then she rolled her eyes back and opened her mouth wide. *LION'S BREATH*, the form was called, and it could push spells and song alike. She raised one foot, slapped her thighs, and let out a shout. The flame burst forward, flying into the hearth.

It reminded Jack of Huangdi, for this was the way dragons projected their fire.

Rosahu stomped, slapped her thighs again, and shouted, each shout rising or falling around a single note. All eyes and ears transfixed on Rosahu. This was our singer, but something still wasn't quite right.

What was missing? She had been masked. Masking changed the voice. She would need to test the theory, but she was right. Of course.

More memories of Huangdi rose, and the alliance she'd proposed with the Sixteen Court. Had she attacked after the refusal? Or helped the court defend against the attack? The details were gone, yet Jack still saw the battle outside the court, earth erupting beneath the gates, and she felt that old mix of fear and rage.

Only when Rosahu stopped did Jack realise the shouts had become a low hum. The song had been driving Jack. Encouraging those memories.

"Where did you learn this?" Jack asked.

Rosahu gestured to Wolfgang, who wrote: *Many visitors came to the ship over the years. Certain knowledge was kept collectively. That's what you told me, yes? And then you practised when the glamour demon didn't interfere?*

Rosahu nodded.

Jack tried to escape the memories and focus on the here and now. The song was good. Now what to make of the difference between Rosahu's voice and the memory from Jack's past visit to the Eldritch?

"Great," Kozak said as a skeleton finished. Wires grew where ligaments might be, and fine hydraulics acted as muscles. "The animation is ready."

Will you paint the masks today? Wolfgang asked.

Jack considered it.

"You must know how much paint you have. Hmm?" Shen Fang asked.

Yes, Jack had an adequate estimation. She could do a practice run without much paint.

We could try act one, Wolfgang said.

"The second animatron is ready," Kozak said. "Third and fourth quick behind it. And I mixed up some enhanced hearing for the tel-fem." Her prosthesis threw a vial to Rosahu.

Rosahu caught it out of the air.

Jack pulled the canvas shard out and let it open, thin crystalline tubes glistening in the fire and winter light. She could use it now. Just for practice. It'd been a long time since she'd painted within one.

"Say, doesn't time and substance step away from a painter in a canvas?" Shen Fang asked. "You don't have the luxury of letting limits slip away from you, do you paintslinger?"

Jack watched the fractals. Just a little wouldn't hurt. Just the masks?

"But what do I know! I'm only a monk," Shen Fang said, beaming.

Fine. Jack gestured, and the canvas folded in on itself, until it was a gem shard. Jack held out her hand, and it settled and adhered to the skin on the back of her hand.

"Ah, you were wise to see what I did not," Shen Fang said.

"Do I get a mask this time?" Kozak asked. "Or are you sticking me in the back as always?"

You chose your contribution before, as you do now.

"Yeah, yeah, whatever, thanks. I do the hard work, and you all get the spotlight. Well put one on Wolfgang, at least. I can't wait to hear her dulcet intonations again."

PAINTSLINGER

Uma Kozak is correct. Will you aid my armour?

"So everyone wants to do this now?" Jack asked. Partially because she knew it required time and others might grow impatient in that time, but also because part of her wanted to do exactly this. Paint. Create. Lose herself in the details of it. Blood still rushed in her ears from Rosahu's song earlier.

Wolfgang gestured, *yes*. Kozak rolled her eyes. Rosahu hesitated, then nodded.

Shen Fang clapped her paws.

"Right. Wolfgang, you're first."

Jack drew her brush and held ready.

CHAPTER ELEVEN

Jack painted reality in front of Wolfgang's mandibles. She used iron white and cobalt black, mixing right in the air. The important thing was not the colour or even the details of the strokes. Jack needed to get the eyes right. Eyes had thresholds that were stepped. They were just shapes, then marbles, then windows into whatever life stood in court.

Wolfgang had eight eyes, and if Jack didn't represent each, Wolfgang would not be able to use this mask. Jack could give extra abilities to the mask, but if she took abilities away, she broke the connection.

"That doesn't look the way I imagined the Eldritch," Shen Fang said.

"It's not supposed to look like the Eldritch," Jack said. "Our masks are part protection, part camouflage. As long as we all look consistent, we won't stand out and harm the story."

Kozak tapped with her prosthesis on her control board. "See, Jack has rules she follows without explaining. This is why I haven't worked with her in hundreds of years. So I'm sure there's some antiquated reason why she won't have you all depicting the Old Ones. But either way, my animatrons will do that near enough."

Jack shaded the areas around the eyes, letting less light

into the inset sockets. Kozak could say what she liked as long as she kept the spark golems working and in line.

"Depiction can destroy as well as create," Jack said.

"I told you. Sounds like a mantra," Kozak said. "So, what? You're so good that if you paint an Eldritch face on Wolfgang, she'll change to being one?"

Jack stepped back. No. The eyes weren't right yet. Approaching the marbles stage, but nowhere near alive.

"Like I said. Rules she doesn't explain," Kozak said.

Almost. The eyes had too much of a sheen on them. Jack mixed in more cobalt.

"Blink," Jack said to Wolfgang.

The mask's eight eyes blinked.

"I didn't know arachnids blinked," Kozak said.

Jack set to work on the outline of the mask. The pale-stretched oval covered Wolfgang's head.

We don't, Wolfgang wrote. *But our masks will share certain similarities. If none of the masks blink, Rosahu or Jack, who both need to blink, wouldn't be able to do so without creating unnecessary contrast between us.*

"Thank you, Wolfgang," Jack said. "Hold still, please. I just need to give you a mouth."

So awkward, Wolfgang wrote.

"Stay still," Jack said.

She complied. Jack added two dots for nostrils and finished with a mouth, mostly humanoid with mandibles at the sides.

"Can you speak?" Jack asked.

Two voices overlaying each other came from the mask's mouth. One very clearly Jack's, the other sounding like a wizened sage.

"I can. Such an awkward experience, this is," Wolfgang said through the mask. The pale oval hung and flowed as though tethered to Wolfgang's head.

Shen Fang clapped again. "She is quite convincing. Why does she sound so?"

"The masks all have a bit of Jack mixed in," Kozak said. "She says its unavoidable, but I think she's just full of herself."

"How're those spark golems coming? I only see five done." Jack wiped her brush on a cloth and moved toward Rosahu.

"You worry about your paint. My animatrons are growing fine," Kozak said.

"Uma Kozak," Wolfgang said through the mask. "You criticise Jack's mask. I wonder, what would a prosthesis of your design sound like? What voice would you give me?"

"It might not be pretty, but it would be unique. One day I'll win you over, Wolfgang," Kozak said.

Jack painted a smaller mask for Rosahu, same pale oval and eight eyes and mandibles at the side of the mouth while Kozak and Wolfgang bantered.

When Jack finished, Rosahu reached up and felt at the paint hanging in front of her face.

"I s ... s-see, differently," Rosahu said. "The mask affects thought."

Jack nodded as she worked.

"Say, am I next?" Shen Fang asked.

"You are indeed," Jack said. "Are you comfortable, Auntie?"

"Oh, I can stand as long as need be. You don't need to worry about this monk. But will I be able to eat with this mask?" Shen Fang asked.

"Yes, but not with the time we have, Auntie," Jack said.

"Hmm. Pity. Alright then. Go on," Shen Fang said.

When Jack finished, Shen Fang turned her head, trying it out.

"Say, this is remarkable." The canine's voice came as a mix of her own and Jacks. She slurred around the arachnid mandibles. "The mask has sensation! I can feel it."

"You do, Auntie," Jack said. "The mask is a part of you for as long as you wear the paint. You feel things at a distance, but you feel them."

"She is correct," Wolfgang said through the mask. "While the mask is armoured, danger to the mask is also danger to the wearer. It is fuelled in part by what we already are."

Jack moved to her duster and dug out her cleaning supplies.

"No mask for you, young paintslinger?" Shen Fang asked.

"Not for this practice run, no," Jack said. "I'll need to use the canvas for my own mask." That mix of dread and excitement rose at the thought. What if she wielded the canvas poorly?

"I'm starting," Kozak said. "Wolfgang, you get the lights, and I'll bring the magic. Well, metaphorically."

Wolfgang looked to Jack.

Jack nodded.

Wolfgang's jade brush out, she cast a darkness ward, drawing the sinuous shapes in ink-like shapes, turbulent at the edges, and the shapes diffused and seemed to drink in the light. The tang of liquorice touched Jack's nose. Wolfgang created another shape, this one blocky and glowing white hot, sent it drifting into the floor at the centre of the room. The liquorice scent vanished under a hint of pollen that made Jack want to sneeze.

Pieces of spark golems, Kozak's animatrons, floated into the light.

Wolfgang replaced the jade brush and moved through the room, drawing hieroglyphs in air. These were not magic wards, but the same technology projections as her calligraphy. Still, they were the symbols of the Eldritch, which, if read too closely, could drive mortals to madness. They could twist the eye and taint the mind. Despite being standard projections, Jack could almost see the catacombs of the Eldritch with these ancient symbols etched in the stone of other stars—

never mind that Wolfgang only drew the shapes and not the walls that held them. Jack would have to paint those herself when the time came. Though some of it would have already been done by past-Jack.

In the light ward at the centre, the spark golems shattered into fragments and swarmed. Pieces of the spark golems collided in air, joined, drifted apart.

The second collision, an arm stayed intact. The third brought a spine.

"Lifter, you can puppeteer the animatrons, now," Kozak said to Shen Fang.

Rosahu cocked her head. Jack moved close to the avatar.

"Do you know this tale?" Jack asked.

Rosahu shook her head.

"The Eldritch were destroyers to such as us," Jack said. "As they died, they travelled in thin places, large mad malices. To stop this, we told them lies: a story from their myths of creation. This is the truce of the Sixteen Court and the Eldritch. When their mind is gone, we recite their myths, and we keep the scattered remains, known as Eldritch tears. Order becomes order. Chaos becomes less."

Jack remembered the final moments in the Eldritch realm, the ocean sky flashed, then the volcanic ash and snow drifted to the darkening world, a moment in her past and in her future.

"That's your explanation?" Kozak asked.

"No, it's the beginning of one," Jack said.

"Listen. Basically, we make giant animatrons that pretend to destroy each other and themselves," Kozak said. "Jack and Wolfgang paint and ward for the setting, and I'm guessing Shen Fang will help puppeteer them. The song and the masks will make the Eldritch see our actions as their myths. Frankly, I'm just there for the giant robot fight."

"And the danger?" Jack asked.

"Easy," Kozak said. "The sky is lava, falling and possibly killing us. And the whole realm is like one big thin place. If we stay, we go crazy, and if we don't, the Old Ones do, and destroy worlds. It's kind of a narrow road, if you see what I mean."

Rosahu nodded, then made a mistake. She moved into the light.

"Rosahu wait," Jack said. "Kozak stop the golems."

Pieces of floating plastique and metal had been swarming now attacked Rosahu.

Rosahu stumbled. And in that moment Jack had two thoughts. One: better for them to fail here than with the Eldritch. And two: they might not be able to pull this off.

Rosahu grew, muscles thickening into chords of flesh. Her mask floated with her changing form.

"Kozak, stop them," Jack said. "Wolfgang, lights."

Wolfgang slashed the jade brush with her forelimb, sending a ward into the space, and the window light filled the room again.

"Kozak," Jack said. Calm.

"Nearly there; put your brush away," Kozak said.

Jack hadn't known she'd drawn it.

Shen Fang moved beside Rosahu.

The floor and walls shook. Surely, the manor wasn't taking offence to these actions?

Rosahu swatted the pieces, grabbed them, broke them. Then two pieces attacked. Shen Fang redirected pieces, but Rosahu was creating more all the time.

"Shall I?" Wolfgang said through the mask, reaching for her sword.

"Kozak?" Jack asked.

"There!" Kozak said.

The golem pieces clattered to the floor. The floor shook again. Paintings rattled against the walls.

"Is the house going to eat us?" Kozak said.

"Why did they attack?" Rosahu said.

"I didn't know you were going to improvise, did I!" Kozak said. "I put this together in an hour. I didn't account for you stepping in the light."

Again, the oak walls vibrated, chandeliers rattling above.

"And what is that!" Kozak said.

"I think," Jack said. "We are under attack."

"This place will attack us?" Shen Fang asked.

A Caravaggio painting fell from the wall. A candelabra tipped.

Jack looked at Wolfgang. Wolfgang looked at Jack. They spoke together.

"Outside."

CHAPTER TWELVE

Wylan Ronde stood on the escarpment overlooking the creator's manse. It looked like Jack's work, though Wylan hadn't crossed paths with that old bore in millennia. Probably an imitator. Still, the strokes were so detailed you couldn't see them if you didn't know how to look. Did that mean there was paint inside for Wylan? Interesting. Good that the dragon had sent her after a painter, then.

The army of stone golems behind her rolled their trebuchets into position. The dragon's insistence on no magic was charming, and perhaps suited the dragon's purposes, but there was nothing like a spell to add that little something extra.

So Wylan walked the lines, warding the stones with exploding runes. This world was far enough away that the dragon wouldn't feel the magic. And if the dragon did, this creator would get the blame. What a wonderful world.

"Pull. Fire. Shoot. Bang!" Wylan said, waving her arms for her own amusement.

The stone golems volleyed the exploding boulders at the walls.

It probably wouldn't work. The manse strokes seemed to suggest a kind of defence mechanism. Maybe that mechanism would fail in time, or even better, the attach would make the manse turn on those inside.

Wylan sat on her palanquin and plucked at her lute.
One way or another, this creator would die.

–•–

Jack had the canvas. She could deal with this in a few strokes.

And, it would likely cost her the last of her paint. No travel to the dying Eldritch. No collaboration with her past self. Madness from the multiple memories. As she tried to think of a way around this, discussion took form around her.

"I can dispatch as many as I am able," Wolfgang said through the mask. "The sword rules this day."

Rosahu grew larger still, now twice as tall as Jack, the oval mask clashing with her huge form.

"Hmm, do you think we would win against such an attack?" Shen Fang asked.

"I've got this," Kozak said.

"You f ... f-fight?" Rosahu asked.

"Me?" Kozak said. "No way. Do these look like warrior arms? I'll send a scout."

Plastic pieces assembled to form a head with a single eye. Three more took shape, so there were four. The four scout golems flew out of the hearth room.

Kozak worked at her desk, and other pieces moved around the chamber. A glamour appeared in the centre of the room. The area outside represented in miniature.

Shen Fang passed her paw through the illusion.

"I haven't added an interface," Kozak said. "Tell me what you want the scouts to show, and I'll move them."

They showed sunset. The estate.

An army. It almost looked like the stone army, but Huangdi would never send them all this way. Yet as volley after volley of exploding rocks smashed into the walls, and the walls reassembled themselves, that conclusion seemed premature. Maybe Huangdi would do just that. Jack pushed down the feeling of betrayal at that. Their past was ancient.

"Someone sits on the brink, watching destruction," Wolfgang said.

"Going," Kozak said. The view swung toward the watcher and the cliff.

A human in a kimono sat on a palanquin. She reclined, plucking some stringed instrument.

A stone golem bumped the palanquin. Piqued, the human turned and drew a ward in the direction of the golem. The golem exploded in chunks that rained on the army and on the human. The human gestured to another golem. That golem raised an umbrella.

"By the horse gods," Kozak said. "Is that Ronde?"

It very much seemed to be. Wylan Ronde, the would-be painter who came too proud to court.

"I thought she was afraid of you, Jack," Kozak said.

The furniture rattled and dust rained under another blast. The dust fell back up into the ceiling.

"I advise we don't fight this battle," Jack said. The canvas rested cool against the back of her hand. How easy it would be. But the paints.

"Good enough. Escape it is," Kozak said. She controlled the scout golems, and they flew up, taking in a wider view of the estate. Stone golems surrounded them. "Or maybe not."

Rosahu's mask wore a troubled face.

The masks. They already wore them. They could go to the Eldritch and now worry about overlapping memories causing madness.

"We escape," Jack said.

Wolfgang moved close to Jack. Yes, she was loyal to a fault.

Even not knowing Jack's plan, she stepped into the fray. This oath wouldn't hold forever. Jack would see to it. Today, though ...

"We escape to the Eldritch Realm," Jack said.

The masks expressed so much. Especially right now. Confusion on Rosahu. Polite concern on Shen Fang. Absolute trust on Wolfgang. Adequate painting in such a short time.

"You crazy ass," Kozak said. "You crazy, insane—"

"I'd almost think you don't remember how to get us there," Jack said.

"Oh, stop smirking. I'll get you there. And back. And then we'll have words."

The view of the army showed an outer wall breach. The ground swallowed the horde until the wall rebuilt itself, but it did so more slowly. The room shook. The mask bearers watched.

"I believe Jack means to paint with the canvas now," Wolfgang said. "And Kozak to help with the spacetime travel."

Jack gave a thumbs-up and put on her duster.

"Kozak, how are you tapping in?" Jack asked.

Kozak held a vial. "Only the good stuff for you, Jack."

Jack walked to the workstation and accepted. She drank. And opened the canvas.

"We would be wise to create space," Wolfgang said.

"What is the drink?" Shen Fang asked.

"This nanodrink creates an interface with Jack's mind and Kozak's equipment," Wolfgang said. "Jack will paint from memory, and Kozak will attempt to triangulate position in the multiverse from Jack's related memories. Time travel is also space travel. This will create a feedback loop where Jack remembers more clearly and can depict more accurately. If she doesn't, we could go to the right space at the wrong time and die in the vacuum of the cosmos."

"What do you mean 'attempt'?" Kozak said. "Get going, Jack."

The army breached a second wall. Two made it into the courtyard. The ground was too slow in swallowing one of them. That golem would be inside soon.

"Rosahu," Jack said.

Rosahu stepped to the entrance of the hearth room. The first golem appeared in the doorway and froze. Something in its stance changed. From puppet to surprised puppeteer. Whoever controlled this thing saw Jack. Jack and, of course, the opening canvas.

Rosahu grabbed the stone golem with one growing hand and smashed it with the other.

"Auntie, may I give you armour?" Jack asked.

Shen Fang didn't answer. She watched the holographic view of the army.

All the army stood still, now. Something made them wait. Not good.

"Auntie?"

The canine's mask swung toward Jack. Worry there, for the first time.

"Armour, for now and for the Eldritch Realm," Jack said. "Broad strokes."

Shen Fang looked at the army, then back to Jack. "As you say, young paintslinger."

Jack worked quickly. Gunmetal black with glints of silver for the reflections. She used her largest brush and brought the amour to curved thorns at shoulders, elbows, and knees.

"Jack," Wolfgang said.

"Yes," Jack said.

"The army is moving." Wolfgang said.

The view showed a new strategy. The front stone golems

drew back but now waited outside the walls for all the others to arrive. They'd come in all at once.

"Guess she's still afraid of you," Kozak said.

"I'd guess so," Jack said. "Rosahu, can you become smaller for this?"

She cycled between male and fem and shrank to Jack's height.

Her armour went on likewise, and in the dim lava light of the Eldritch Realm, they'd be invisible to the attention of the Old Ones. Hopefully.

Wolfgang stood patiently while Jack augmented the arachnid armour already in place.

Jack looked to Kozak. "May I provide armour for you, Uma Kozak? It doesn't approach the crafts of the equine, but—"

"Skip the ceremony. I know our kind of armour wouldn't last there. Do it."

Jack painted Kozak's armour, then. The curved horns, where the mane would be, gave the whole piece a feeling of sculpture more than armour.

"Don't just stand there admiring your own work. Get moving," Kozak said.

Jack lowered her goggles and stepped into the canvas cage. The fractal portal moved as a Mandelbrot evolution with an interior that Jack stood inside. Jack lifted her hands like a knight awaiting gauntlets. The crystalline shards appeared at her left, the crystalline bristles at her right.

Jack dipped the fine bristles in her bandolier cartridges. She imagined the crystal shape at her left as a mirror. It vanished, and as Jack painted in front of her, the armour appeared on her own body. As she painted the mask, the white oval covered her face.

Masked and armoured, Jack set about creating the Eldritch Realm. She'd start on the canvas shards, then pull the canvas surface away and paint on reality. It wasn't necessary, but it had been a long time. The mirror returned to her left hand, and she began with crimson.

"Jack," Kozak said, "the army is moving again. They're storming together."

Jack plied the brush to the flat shard. The bristles bucked like a mechanical machine with too much torque. Had it always been this difficult? Jack tried again, and the crimson refused to stick. A vibration thrummed up the bristles and into Jack's arm. Nausea began to sink in.

"The stone golems come," Wolfgang said.

So they did.

Jack tried again. One splodge of crimson stuck and sparks flew off in a magnetic arc of light like a miniature solar flare.

A stone golem ran into the room, then another and a third. Rosahu and Wolfgang moved among them, smashing stone and sending great clouds of pulverised rock through the musty air.

Focus, Jack.

What was the painful part? Never good to start that way, but better there than nowhere.

The falling lava sky.

The bristles moved, and the paint stuck. Welding sparks came off the strokes, and that was alright. Once more, the canvas fought and the bristles bucked but Jack pressed the paint. In her painting, the crimson became lava rain falling with contrail clouds behind. Huge meteors fell from the lava sky creating thin places—wrong places where shadows were too deep and gap crossers preyed on the unwary travellers.

Jack remembered that falling sky. The dying god that took with it so much of what it meant to be a knight in the Sixteen Court. That last piece of who Jack had been. The god died and took a piece of Jack with it.

"I'm getting it," Kozak said. "Keep going!"

Jack was vaguely aware of the room. Framed paintings gathered from across time and space clattered to the marble, destroyed in the sacrilege of Wylan's attack. Dust pelted Jack as stone golems fell under Wolfgang's sword and Rosahu's fists. But these wounds must be kept distant, or Jack would get lost in the harm of the present rather than that of the past.

Jack removed the canvas shards. The paint stayed floating. Jack moved to the black spaces, painting the cyclopean ruins that cut across that lava sky, jutting into it and never reaching the heights that marked the gods' abode. In the maze of those ruins, Jack had stood while the Eldritch wept. But Jack hadn't cried. She couldn't. The feelings weren't hers to possess, then. The tears wanted to come, but couldn't. Jack had been dry in the lava rain.

"Jack!" Kozak shouted.

The picture was real, now. A three dimensional painting became a three dimensional hole in reality, and through the hole, the Eldritch realm shone red. But it was static. Jack had to bring it to life. She painted pieces of the manor around them flying into the portal in reality, sucked by the pressure differential. She slashed her brush again and again, frantic, droplets flying. She painted, her arm aching, the view becoming more real, and golems flew past her brushes into the hole, sucked into a living painting that had become a portal. Jack painted more.

"Jackson," Wolfgang said through the mask.

Jack slashed again, and again, more and more.

"It is enough," Wolfgang said.

Jack forced herself to stop and see. The oak wall splintered, and the plaster peeled, ripping and tearing at the seams, tugging toward the ten metre hole in reality.

Apparently, everyone waited for her.

PAINTSLINGER

"Wolfgang," Jack said and gestured.

Wolfgang jumped through. Rosahu went after. Shen Fang glided through, seeming to float.

"You coming or not?" Kozak shouted over the din.

"She ruined this place," Jack said.

"Oh hell," Kozak said. "Don't use too much paint!" With that she leapt through.

CHAPTER THIRTEEN

Wylan watched as the manor began imploding, her lute hanging at her side.

She had only a moment to wonder at this, as the east wall blew out toward Wylan, pulverising stone golems and everything between the manor and Wylan's vantage on the rocky hill.

Impossible. Jack had a canvas.

Time for a quick illusion? Yes, she thought it was.

But Wylan was wrong. The ground lifted below her, raking her clothes and ripping at her skin.

-•-

Jack painted the cliff exploding. Wylan had survived worse, but hopefully it sent the message clearly.

Jacked turned and jumped through into the Eldritch Realm.

On the other side, the hole hung three dimensional, but too large. Jack had gone too far. The size brought through her manor house in tatters, debris pluming and bursting into the portal and erupting out through the spherical hole in reality.

Jack ran, the planks and plaster hitting her back, almost sending her to the ground. The others ran ahead of her into the blackened ruins. Shen Fang looked back and stopped.

She turned and ran toward Jack. Then her running steps became bounds. Then, she disappeared and reappeared in front of Jack. She grabbed Jack and pulled. The canvas followed.

Debris pelted Jack's armour and Shen Fang's. Jack tried to run like Shen Fang, but each time her feet touched, they dragged. How?

And then they weren't running so much as skipping forward in space, appearing further and further ahead of the destruction in glitch jumps of consciousness. Not good if Jack was going dark.

Shen Fang stopped beside the turret.

"Say," she said. "That seemed hasty!"

"Yes Auntie, it was hasty," Jack said.

"It still is! Look."

Jack looked. The hole had become an eruption. The sediment and cliff around the castle of there compounded with bedrock and silt of here. The hole hadn't brought just the manor, but a chunk of the planet's crust. Explosion followed explosion, pressure growing then bursting upward again in plumes. More of the other reality there came through.

Wolfgang came out of the gigantic doorway set in the turret ruins. Kozak spoke from inside the turret without looking up from her equipment.

"I told you," Kozak said.

"You told me not to use too much paint," Jack said. "I was sparing."

"Liar," Kozak said.

"Fair," Jack admitted.

"How?" Rosahu asked in that strange mix of Jack's voice and her own. She pointed to Shen Fang.

Yes. Good point. How had Shen Fang rescued Jack?

Shen Fang's mask beamed. "I'm not so old I can't jog a little, hmm!"

"Did I go weak?" Jack asked.

Shen Fang leaned close. "You touch reality when you paint. There are other ways to touch reality, young one. I helped you along when you needed it."

Indeed, and so she had. Definitely not just a patron, then.

The eruptions became intermittent. A small mountain now stood geysering rock at odd intervals, and surprisingly, it looked familiar.

Jack had seen the other side of it. The barrier from the past.

Far above, kilometres or more, beyond sulphur wisps, the water sky rippled in an oceanic shell. In the deeps of the ocean sky, the Eldritch swam, lava forms now that erstwhile coalesced into the forms of destruction known to so many civilisations throughout time.

"They aren't b … b-beings?" Rosahu asked.

"No," Jack said. "This Old One took smaller shapes at times, and this rock played host to the shapes. Some say it was how they reproduced, others how they travelled. We only know that when they die, they take shape, travel, and destroy. Their deaths cause great havoc. In their lives, they knew this. The story, order from chaos, is an older story, and giving them a part in the story would restrain them, of their own design." The story only paintslingers and artists could realise for them.

The Eldritch came to this strange place where rock bleached below a sky with liquid water instead of clouds. And in the liquid sky, lava flows moved, casting the only light in this place. In the distance, the water sky exploded in billows of huge steam and lava fell, contrails falling behind, a piece of the dying god. Thunder came to them a few seconds later. It echoed farther here under the liquid layer of atmosphere. It reminded Jack of a standing on a volcano as it erupted. There on the volcano's verge, the heat and the lava rain were the whole of reality.

Rosahu pointed. A piece of lava broke free of the water surface and fell in billowing trails to the far side of the barrier of destruction Jack had brought through. She shivered.

The others did the same. They'd be feeling it now, too.

"You may feel uncomfortable," Jack said. She motioned at the stone ruins around them on the bleached rock. "You might feel like the world is thin in these ruins, and that there is something you can do to make it thicker. You aren't wrong, but that is not why we're here."

Would Kozak have a wisecrack here? A joke to make light?

No, she worked at her portable machine, already regrowing itself after the travel.

This moment imprinted itself on Jack's mind. Everyone in their armour under the lava sky. Each ready to gift the Old One a good end. Even in the thin places.

A good day, then.

This should be easier than before, as her past self, with past Kozak and past Wolfgang, did the bulk of the work. They'd probably have to depict more of the gap crossers, pick at the creations of those others as Kozak's spark golems had attacked Rosahu.

A huge explosion shattered the side of the debris mountain, and someone climbed out and slid down the scree. At first Jack thought it her own doing, but she realised a tone came through the distance. It sounded like a lute.

Wylan Ronde had come through to the Eldritch Realm.

CHAPTER FOURTEEN

Smells of sulphur drifted into the rubble.

Wylan tried to move.

The stone golems had thrown themselves on her, taking care not to crush her. Just as well. They'd failed spectacularly with Jack.

Jack, the ancient, cocky, self-absorbed creator had tried to kill Wylan Ronde, Bard to the Man Emperor.

Except she'd had a canvas. If she'd really wanted to kill Wylan, Wylan wouldn't be here now, thinking this.

Never mind.

"Free my hand," Wylan said.

A stone golem began to smash another that lay across her casting arm. Ah, the one doing the smashing was not a golem. It was that stupid feline that'd had come with news of the other canvas. Now that she was a stone prisoner, she'd survived this far, had she? Almost worth destroying just for the fun of it, but the feline actually served better than the idiotic golems.

"Put your tail into it, sweetheart," Wylan said.

Her arm came loose and she could cast, yet ...

Jack would see if Wylan got out. Who cared! Not Wylan. Never Wylan. Wylan feared no being.

But she may as well get clear without making a fuss. Just clever business, really.

PAINTSLINGER

"You. Shield me," she said to the feline.

The stone prisoner did as she was told, of course. Wylan threw a small concussion ward. The crushing debris exploded outward.

"Come on then," Wylan said. She might need a body to absorb attacks. The stone feline nodded.

Wylan climbed free and ran for cover.

--•--

Jack watched as, beyond the mountain of debris, past-Jack painted the tops of turrets and spires, completing them, hiding the ruins they'd become.

Not too sloppy, actually. The technique was rough but inspired. Oh, okay one stroke was bad. Scale was correct but too much flourish. Had Jack ever been so brash? So blunt?

Good thing she'd learnt to be humble. She'd grown far humbler.

Before, Kozak hadn't grown spark golems. Her machinations had been almost clockwork, gears and pistons. The clockwork giants began as 'chaos', independent pieces that moved through the cyclopean spires and past-Jack painted those spires as the Eldritch imagined their prehistory.

And then some of the paint came free.

On this side of the destruction mount, Wylan's silhouette cast wards against the paint.

Too far. Jack would end her now. She'd die in their past for her desecration.

Except the act of murder would desecrate this place just as much as Wylan's obstinacy.

So, this was the nature of their duel, then? Jack had to create where past-Jack had created faster than Wylan could unpick it?

Another lava ball burst through the ocean sky and fell past the giant clockwork golems. A bright sound, like a bird-call, chirruped from the ruins behind Jack. Another.

Rosahu started to move in that direction.

"Hold, singer," Jack said.

Rosahu paused.

"There are things in those ruins that will lull you. Note the darkness there. It isn't merely a lack of light. Stay where you can see and seek no sound nor smell that isn't known."

Rosahu nodded.

"Find a safe location and sing for your life, then. For all of ours."

Rosahu nodded again.

"Kozak, let Shen Fang drive your spark golems as you did in the manor. Auntie, you know the story. Please tell the parts that need telling."

"Wolfgang, between your symbols, will you protect those as need protecting? Face the nightmares of this place with darkness of your own?"

The arachnid hunched and drew her sword.

Jack moved into the turret and ran up the steps.

Several times the stairwell offered two paths with one seeming a little too shadowed. Another path had a malevolent drip in its corner, a drip splatting in a pattern that was some sort of language Jack could almost understand if she only stopped, investigated, explored. Jack stayed the course, though. Such snares were not for her kind.

Better to be at a high place for what came next.

At the ragged top of the turret, Jack stood. The sulphur clouds surrounded her here, and the ocean sky above churned. Lava refracted through its depths and threw caustic shafts of red light to the planet's surface and ruins.

The canvas still open around her, Jack raised her brush

hand. She'd take no palette or surface, just now. With the canvas, she could paint the space beyond the mountain of rubble. If she kept the paint to the clockwork golems themselves, past-Jack might not notice. She had been self-absorbed then, unlike now. Obviously. Fine crystal bristles appeared. Jack dipped into the colours of her bandolier. She looked at the texture of reality in the distance, and she plied her brush, imagining the paint there.

Sparks burst from the place in the distance, the place where Wylan had stripped paint from the clockwork golems. The paint still stuck to the bristles. It hadn't worked, and already her arm ached. She waited for the headache to come from overlapping memories, but none rose. Had she really been so myopic?

Enough thinking and try again, Jack.

She did, and the sparks arced and lit Wylan's shape on the mount of rubble. Paint still marked the bristles. No clashing memories splintered her mind.

A flaw appeared in the clockwork giant's side. Inside the huge golem where paint and metal flaked, pendulums swung visible and huge. This was as she remembered. This was when she'd noticed the other party. Past-Jack would see present-Jack.

Come on, Jack. No distractions. For the Eldritch and the lost Sixteen Court.

She pushed with all the strength in her arm. Light flared. The gap in paint was patched—the clockwork golem of the Old One's bodily shape whole once again.

Wylan threw something toward Jack. Jack painted it gone, light flaring and bursting with each stroke.

Wylan turned and attacked the illusion of the spires. Jack painted them whole.

Wylan stopped.

Present-Kozak's new spark golems rose, swarming and feigning attack on the old giants and Jack saw why Wylan had stopped.

She was changing Kozak's spark golems. They weren't just feigning attack, now, but actually trying to pull the old giants apart. Jack saw it happening and moved in one.

Her past-self had noticed another party and kept painting. This was comforting to share the effort, yet it also meant everything else was up to present-Jack. Past-Jack painted the ruins, detailed the golems, told the old tales. Present-Jack did everything else.

A memory of her brief meeting with herself rose, but too soon. She had to focus or Wylan—

One of the swarming golems exploded, crippling the clockwork machine.

Before the cloud of debris flew out, Jack painted the debris gone. Not enough. The giant canted. Sweat broke out under the mask, as Jack painted for her life. Pieces of the machine that would fit. Whole new sections.

Wolfgang's symbols drifted into place and implied rune-covered tablets and murals. Jack filled in the space behind them to show the maze this place had once been.

Yet something was missing. Jack could still see the pieces of the ruse.

Jack listened. No song.

From the height of the turret, Jack looked below, searching the ruins for Rosahu. In the red light, Jack caught motion below. Wolfgang moved as a dark blur around a pale form. Jack saw the stance, wide legs and arms, moving from breathing pose to breathing pose, but no sound reached Jack.

Instead of painting ruins above, Jack threw the charcoal black beyond Rosahu. A wall of amphitheatre rose with the slashes, and a faint echo of shouts and chant reached Jack's

PAINTSLINGER

ears. Too faint. Another slash upward, and a third, again and again, until Rosahu stood in a half-basin, and sound bounced toward Jack and up beyond her.

For half a second, Jack heard the notes themselves and resigned all as lost.

Memory aligned, then. Jack remembered her thoughts in the past, almost word for word.

"This is the end of the court."

And she'd been right. The planet and location of the Sixteen Court had been gone for centuries by that time. Yet, oaths prolonged the fiction of artist warriors. This was the last oath, and she'd known it, even then.

And as she'd thought before, she thought now. If this was an end, let it be a good one.

She turned back to Wylan's blows and undoings and painted. With each blur of colour she let fly in the red light, she remembered this ending and the others before. When Wylan left the court in disgrace and battle. Even Huangdi. Everything ended.

Some part of Jack realised that Rosahu's magic worked even now. Jack's heart brought her own pains to this song, filled it in, as each person no doubt did and as the Eldritch would do. Thoughts of paint and spark, song and rune drifted into the recesses of her mind. At the forefront, like a chant: this was an end. Let it be a good one.

But it did not end. Not yet.

Jack painted. Both Jacks. The singer sang. And the lie was made true.

Jack threw stroke after stroke, while lava burst through the ocean sky in slanted pillars of fire. Together they lied to the dying god, told them they mattered, that they were forever, that their gifts would outlive them, while everyone knew the truth of Rosahu's song.

All things end.

Wylan attacked with golems, and Jack countered, sweating with the creation of it. But the end neared.

In the story they told, it was tie for the final attack, sending chaos—or in this case—pieces of metal and wire. It all moved as one against the three clockwork golems. The clockwork golems reached their piston arms with jets of gas escaping at joints and captured Kozak's new animatrons, pulling them out of their flight and hurling them to the rocky surface below. They moved their arms as though shaping new turrets and towers atop the fallen animatrons, and Jack slashed the paint, making their motions true. She hurled colour after colour, filling in the sky with spires where their hands moved.

Here, Wylan should have known the story. Her efforts, instead of obstructing Jack, actually helped. A single ward rose, glowing in the dim haze, and touched the copper head of the nearest clockwork golem. It shook, and shuddered, and began tearing at itself and its surroundings.

The golems tore at each other, mad with destruction, and crumbled upon the firmament they'd built. Creators died, but if they were lucky, as in this story, the creations might live on.

Jack lowered her brush for a moment and took in the sights and sounds, the giant shapes she'd created with friends past and present, and even with an enemy. A good end, and a creation made.

The sky flashed, lava burned bright and cast the entire asteroid in relief. Jack squinted, and when vision returned, she saw the final piece of lava falling, distant in the sudden cold quiet. It seemed to take an age to reach the planet's surface, and the sound was small, and far.

Fog descended in cloudy wisps. A single snowflake drifted in front of Jack, then a second snowflake. With no lava above, this place would soon be given to the lurkers in the shadows.

PAINTSLINGER

Jack waited, feeling the end of it. Starting again always felt wrong, like it cheapened what came before. Still, start again, she must.

Jack painted a single pale glowing orb above both parties, remembering it from both perspectives. And as falling snow thickened in the light of her orb, orange flares twinkled, like stars among the snow, drifting down to Jack and, no doubt, to everyone else here.

The tears of the Eldritch. Their gifts.

Orange gifts drifted to the others, and Jack saw what she should have seen before. A gift also fell to Wylan in the distance.

Disgust rose like bile at the desecration of it, and Jack brought the brush to bear and painted hard. Blinding arcs flashed. The force shook her entire painting arm, and a perfect black cube glistened where Wylan had been. A geometric prison for a hack of an artist. Jack would deal with Wylan and her stolen gift shortly. Let her wait in trepidation for her judgement.

For now, there was one more thing to do. Should she? No. But could she resist? Likewise, a no. She already remembered this clearly. It had already happened. Such a moment wouldn't cause madness.

Jack painted a portal to the other side of the mountain. The strokes were fast and rough but effective. Jack stepped through and stood in front of her past-self, expecting to find companionship, another lost knight.

"Hail, paintslinger," Jack said.

Her younger self in cruder armour cocked her head and gave a salute. Jack remembered being that person. A little more sure of herself, yet only because she didn't know herself as well as she did now. And the pain of this ritual under all that. Seeing herself gave no solace or companionship. This was an incomplete person with foolish mistakes still to be made.

"You did well," Jack said, finally.

"Not bad, anyway. A fitting end," young-Jack said.

"A fitting end. You served your Court well," Jack said.

"Is the Secret kept?" young-Jack asked.

A chill went through Jack. The greeting of one paintslinger to another after the destruction of the Court.

"Safely kept," Jack said.

"I'll ask no questions," young-Jack said. She gestured to the evolving fractal frame of the canvas.

"I'll tell no lies," Jack lied. "Give my best to Wolfgang and Kozak."

Young-Jack seemed taken aback with that. Of course. She'd think them dead.

"And I'll do the same for you?"

"If you please," young-Jack said.

"Travel well," Jack said, and she stepped through her hole in reality back to the top of the turret.

There, she painted it gone.

The others stood atop the turret, too.

"I'm sure that's forbidden," Shen Fang said. "Speaking to your past-self. Preserved time lines and so on?"

"I'm sure it is, Auntie," Jack said. "Report me to your nearest knight of the Sixteen Court."

"Can we get out of here?" Kozak asked. "I heard a voice I knew in the ruins."

"I have to deal with the lazy one first," Jack said.

"Lazy one?" Wolfgang asked through the mask.

"The artist who tears others' work down and thinks herself a creator because she understands of the tools."

"Ronde," Kozak said.

"Wylan Ronde," Jack agreed.

PAINTSLINGER

Outside the monolithic cube, Jack painted a seam in the surface and touched it. The door retracted into the wall and disappeared. She had seen such things on Train-Man worlds.

Jack stepped to the side. "Wylan Ronde, you have jeopardised a past event beyond all law, and you've risked the last fulfilment of the Eldritch Pact. Come forth with all instruments of art and music laid bare." She paused, then forced herself to finish. "Cry mercy and you shall have it."

An earthy sound came from the space. Jack threw a paint light inside.

The walls and ceiling still shone black as expected, and the earth still sat scorched. All but the corner.

Wylan was not hiding. She was gone. Long vines were left behind. The Eldritch Tear took the shape of the gift you desired. Wylan, wasteful and lazy, had already used hers, it seemed.

"We know what her gift was," Jack said to her companions. "Come on in, those as would see with your own eyes."

Rosahu and Shen Fang entered.

"A call to the goodvines," Jack said. "Not as rare as a canvas, but a worthy gift indeed."

"Oh my," Shen Fang said. "We've let her loose in the past."

"No," Jack said. "The goodvines cross space and time. Grow across it, really. When need is great or the call is used. These goodvines are from our present."

"How do you know?" Shen Fang asked.

"Because they know," Jack said. "Old myths talked of world trees or life trees, and for a long time, folks took that for the babble of the primitive. But there are malevolent things that cross the gaps between worlds, and there are good things that grow in dark places, much to their misfortune. The goodvines can't do much, but they may provide escape to a timeline they recognise. Time's banyan trees know whence they grow."

Rosahu advanced and knelt beside the tunnel of dead branches. She touched it and a twig broke off. Rosahu held the twig up in the light.

Jack knelt beside Rosahu. "Dead. Wylan killed it after it saved her."

"What are you doing in there? It's getting cold," Kozak said.

"Then come inside. And be ready for a tight squeeze," Jack said.

"She's crazy you know?" Kozak said.

"As you say, Uma Kozak," Wolfgang said.

"Why do they call you crazy?" Shen Fang asked.

"Because we're going to give chase. Secure your Eldritch gifts and prepare yourselves. We'll catch Wylan and stop her laziness."

"And stop her killing, right?" Kozak asked.

"That too," Jack said. She crawled into the twisted root tunnel.

CHAPTER FIFTEEN

Wylan arrived at the dragon court. Her ripped kimono hung limp in the dead air, and the dumb feline puppet in no way kept up with Wylan's needs on the road.

Oh, and all the worlds kept turning to stone. The feline puppet navigated the bardo worlds well enough, but Wylan hadn't agreed to turn everything in all the worlds to dead rock. No, she had become Bard to the dragon who wanted to escape samsara, and then when the dragon died, Wylan would do whatever she wanted. Namely, take over the kingdom as Bard Emperor and dig up all the toys she'd accrued in service of the dragon. The canvas, and now this new gift of an Eldritch tear.

But not on this world. Wylan would live on a world with far more ... luxuries. This place offered few amenities suitable for a person of her sophistication. A skilled bard deserved far more than buildings in disrepair with only broken minds to amuse her.

Look at this place.

The gate hung blackened but serviceable and swung open all the same. All the way through, it looked like flame demons had danced and frolicked. The menagerie, too, glistened blackly in the pale light.

When she became empress of the worlds, she would do

away with this rock of a world for good. In the meantime ...

"You. Go stand where you're supposed to." The feline complied and became the only non-burnt statue in the array.

In the throne room, the scorched tapestries marked the walls and one of the support pillars had crumpled. Yet, the far wall of twisted thorns looked like deadwood, and the man-doll mask lifted its head up and smiled.

"Hello, Bard," the voice said. Well now, wasn't that something. The voice came from the doll.

"My Emperor is faring well, I see," Wylan said.

"My Bard less so. And my court." The doll gestured. "But we've found a way to stop after all. Thanks to you."

Wylan bowed a thank you. Never mind that she had no idea what the dragon spoke of. Praise was praise. And well-deserved, after all.

"Yes, you extend my peace, now. Across all the neighbouring worlds, where you go, our gift of escape goes with it. Magic fails where you are. Indeed, you'd have to go quite far to get away from my peace. Further than you like." The doll examined its puppet hand. Was it being coy?

"The Emperor is gracious with gifts. I shall rest and recover, then perhaps we can see to repair in this place. For the sake of your honour."

The man doll shook its head.

"My emperor?" Wylan asked.

"No. Such would be creation. Creation and destruction both extend the cycle of samsara. The court stays as it is. It reminds me to keep my peace when your efforts fail. The creator you chase caused quite a stir before you intervened. I felt much magic."

"A troublesome foe," Wylan said.

"And one well handled, Bard. But no rest waits for you here. Take from the stone ones and go. Spread my peace."

PAINTSLINGER

"Of course. Perhaps after I resupply—"

The doll put hands on knees and leaned forward. The black eyes peered through Wylan.

"Silly me," Wylan said. "I meant I'd resupply as I travelled, Emperor."

"Fare well, Bard. When the neighbouring worlds and their neighbouring worlds to their borders all know my peace, the court awaits your return. I shall escape samsara, and you shall be free of your oath."

"A sad day, Emperor."

"I'm sure you'd say so, Bard."

More travel after all, then. Thank the bodhisattvas for that feline. And after the dragon in the man mask died, Wylan would mix paint and use the canvas. Wylan would become a paintslinger.

--•--

Jack emerged from the long warren of dry roots to a stone ground, not paved but changed, petrified into stone the shape of dirt.

The huge banyan trees should be greeting her, offering succour and shelter, yet the trees hung dead against a winter sky. They towered up and swayed no more.

Jack stepped out of the canvas and let it fold in on itself. It attached to the back of her hand once more.

"Horses don't crawl," Kozak said, emerging. "I want to make that clear. No more time travel that way. Oh wow."

"Not good," Rosahu said.

"As you say, singer," Jack said. "These were sentient."

"My mask is becoming stiff," Wolfgang said.

Jack nodded and began preparing paint thinner on a cloth. She had to remove the paint masks and armour before it limited their motions or abilities. She started with herself, then removed Wolfgang's mask.

When Shen Fang came free and stepped into this world, Jack used the thinner on a cloth and removed Shen Fang's armour and mask, then Kozak's.

"That cloth smells awful," Kozak said.

It does have a certain acerbic quality, Wolfgang wrote, now that she had no mask.

"This is a great crime," Shen Fang said. "This is why we need your help, paintslinger."

The canine was correct. Jack kept waiting for some movement or calligraphy from the sapient plants. If this was permanent, Wylan had moved from attempted murder to genocide. "I'll set up over there and mix," Jack said. "With the tear of the Eldritch, I should once again have paint to outlast the stars."

I shall explore, Wolfgang said.

"I'm with her. I don't like being in the middle of this place," Kozak said.

Shen Fang and Rosahu followed Jack to a covering of branches that almost made a room. Shen Fang sat outside in the lotus position and meditated. Rosahu stood guard.

Good enough.

Jack donned goggles and mask, pulled gloves from buttoned pockets, and laid out a flat piece of synthetic cloth on the ground. The cloth hardened into a mixing surface. Non-porous and level.

The pigment, the base, and the tear of the Eldritch came together. Jack used the pestle and a palette knife, then mixed, filling her cartridges as she went.

As she worked, she let her mind wander.

This was her routine, and it helped her work out larger problems. For example, Wylan Ronde. How had she gone from being an obsequious art critic to actively jeopardising time travel and the rituals of the paintslingers? She had wanted to be a paintslinger. She'd come to the Sixteen Court and stood before the knights and proclaimed her loyalty. That had been near the end. Endless war across universes had been at the brink of the court, and some had wanted to take Wylan in. Including Jack.

Jack had been younger and a little less aware. The praise had seemed genuine, and mayhap it had been. Yet this was the problem with those as would drive another person's actions. Sometimes they did so accidentally, stroking the parts of a soul because it stroked their own soul in like manner. It was impossible to know the why of it, even for the person doing the praising.

Jack had seen it, in the end. Wylan's desire to move to the higher arts without the work in the lower. That could be forgiven and worked out. But when Jack stopped responding to Wylan's praise—that befitting a knight and teacher artist— Wylan had changed from praise to ridicule. Even this could be forgiven. But when the first knight offered Wylan the guidance and given her the option delaying her teaching, Wylan had been insulted.

Then she had attacked the court. A promising display of what skills she had learnt in those months among masters, and not damning in and of itself. No, what made her unfit to be a painter knight was her unwillingness to look at herself critically, to admit that deliberately or not, she had acted in a way she had agreed she wouldn't.

An artist who could not look critically at herself was only an art critic, a shade of a creator rather than a creator god.

The cartridges sat filled in a circle. Jack began to mix the tear now with the pigment itself. This would allow future mixes to benefit from the odd self-replication and made endless paint possible.

And Jack? Was she now the epitome of the painter knight?

No. Her hands went through the motions and the rituals of her kin, but she was a rogue now, a professional liar. She might do some good for Shen Fang and the canines, but the kingdom was gone. Lost to time. And the secret meant it would never come back, never be tapped again for its near limitless experience and wisdom.

Better for the canine folk than for the Sixteen Court, and dead kingdom in a dead universe.

She—

The white pigment ran out. Even mixed with the tear of the Eldritch.

Impossible. Unless the gift demon had cursed her supply? Was a gift demon so powerful as to override the will of the Eldritch? Such magic didn't exist anymore, except perhaps among the dragon kin. Huangdi lived worlds away and remained intent on dying. There was no way to extend the magic so far without someone carrying it.

So the gift demon lied twice. Once in giving her the endless paint. Twice in tainting all future attempts at making the paint.

Jack tidied the mess and stepped outside.

Shen Fang opened her eyes. "Some would guess you suffer, young paintslinger. Why do we suffer?"

"Attachment, Auntie," Jack said by rote. Not a good time for a lecture.

"Perhaps we will take tea in this new catacomb?" Shen Fang said.

Translation: make me tea, youngling. "I'm afraid my implements are not with me. I have only the herbs, not the kettle."

Besides, there was no time. She needed to figure out how to get to the gift demon.

"Say, our friend Uma Kozak could probably grow a kettle from almost nothing!" Shen Fang said. "Perhaps Rosahu would seek Uma Kozak for us?"

Rosahu nodded and turned.

"Sit. Breathe," Shen Fang said. "Humour an old monk."

Jack did as she was asked.

"Something is not as you expect," Shen Fang said.

"You aren't wrong. I might have to return your canvas."

"Sure! Or you could find what's causing this unexpected turn and rectify it. Isn't that what paintslingers do?"

"Auntie—"

"Do you know the story of the flower sermon?"

Right. No getting out of this. Jack nodded on the chance the canine would leave it or get to her point.

"After the awakened one died, followers argued about the teachings. Were the words the important part of his teachings? Or did the awakened one, by being aware of the nature of reality, give these words their enlightened meaning?" Shen Fang frowned. "Listen to an old monk, will you?"

"Yes Auntie."

"In the flower sermon, we have an answer. It is said the awakened one held up a lotus flower to the disciples. Thousands of monks gathered, and nuns and gods from many universes. One person there smiled. That smiling disciple understood that words could not always convey the beauty of reality. Words can carry so much, but they take time to lead a student to enlightenment. Certain messages can be conveyed in an instant. The unexpected fullness of the lotus flower."

Jack looked up. Shen Fang floated a metre above the ground, hovering with legs crossed in the lotus position. Light shone from her forehead to Jack, and Jack saw herself floating above a battlefield.

A memory? No. Jack didn't do battle. Battle was for heroes. Jack created. Jack travelled.

The floating Jack of the vision had light pouring from her. Jack blinked. Shen Fang sat on the ground.

"Rosahu! You've returned. Thank you for serving an old monk."

Rosahu began setting a fire and a kettle.

Shen Fang smiled and leaned toward Jack. Her voice was low and gravelly in the way that canine voices became when they whispered. "You found something unexpected, yes? Be glad. Reality is unexpected. In such moments, we can know the nature of reality, and so can others. We can gift awakening in the unexpected."

Shen Fang leaned back, closed her eyes, and smiled, every measure the happy monk.

Rosahu served tea in Kozak's creations until Kozak and Wolfgang returned at nightfall.

The stone spreading stops two kilometres away, Wolfgang wrote. *It grows, but slowly. The trees there are retreating.*

"As much as I want to blame Ronde," Kozak said. "This doesn't feel like her."

Jack still went over the image Shen Fang had given her, somehow. Paintslingers touched reality directly. It wasn't often they discovered something new.

"Jack?" Rosahu said.

"Go on," Jack said.

"Not much more to say," Kozak said. "Ronde teamed up with Huangdi a while back. Now before you get defensive Jack, hear me out."

"Huangdi wants to die," Jack said. "Not kill the goodvines. Not kill anyone. Huangdi cannot create or destroy. She would prolong herself."

Shen Fang seemed more interested all of a sudden. Less jolly.

"I'll grant you that Huangdi can be extreme," Jack said. "Being reborn as a dragon has made her volatile."

"Huangdi was always volatile," Kozak said, "and the dragon suits her fine which is why she'll live forever as one. You are the first to defend, Jack. But I notice you didn't get Huangdi's help with the Eldritch. Face it. Huangdi isn't all cherry blossoms to be around."

"A friend," Rosahu said. She meant to stick up for Jack, which was kind but perhaps not the best time.

"Hold, Rosahu. Kozak, I'm not qualified to say what Huangdi can or can't do or be. That's up to her."

"Pardon, young paintslinger," Shen Fang said. "There is a dragon threatening our world hub. Stone golems raid day and night. These are space ships in orbit that send small landing parties that attack our cities. We think they are skirmishes, but likely the beginning of something much larger. Maybe you should look there for the unexpected."

"What unexpected?" Kozak asked. "Ah damn, what's gone wrong now?"

May as well tell them all.

"The Eldritch tear didn't work. Not completely. So, I'll run out of paint again. The gift demon lied, and is still lying. Even new paint runs out."

"You blame the gift demon, but perhaps it's related to this?" Shen Fang gestured to the petrified banyan trees looming around them.

"Huangdi is not a murderer," Jack insisted.

"Not as you expect," said Shen Fang.

"Pardon, Auntie, but you seem focused on me going after Huangdi. Why did you not mention these raids when you first offered me the canvas?"

Jack, Wolfgang said.

"No no, brushmaster. She is right. The truth has layers,

and she's discovered a new one. I knew she'd refuse to fight the dragon in the man mask. My fellow monks will face the dragon when the time comes. We will finish our world hub and end that threat ourselves. But who could face the Bard? Who had personal knowledge of how to defeat Wylan Ronde?"

"A paintslinger," Kozak said.

"Lies," Rosahu said.

Truth. And Jack didn't disagree with any of it.

"So," Jack said, "this is the real reason I have a canvas. To defeat Wylan Ronde and let you challenge Huangdi?"

Shen Fang nodded.

"If you find that Huangdi isn't behind this," Jack gestured. "Will you let her be?"

She nodded again.

"Do you give oath to the Sixteen Court on penalty of justice?"

Strong words. But warranted.

Shen Fang leaned back, considered, then nodded. "I give oath, paintslinger. And I cry pardon for any omissions you find deceitful."

"No Auntie, I don't begrudge you your motives. But I won't go after Wylan with diminishing paint."

They all stared at Jack. As well they might.

"I'm going to cross the worlds and find the lying gift demon," Jack said.

"Not tonight though, right?" Kozak asked.

Jack considered.

Jackson.

"Okay. On the morn. Sleep fast and wake ready."

Jack waited for everyone to walk away and make camp before approaching Kozak's self-manufacturing gazebo.

"Hail, maker," Jack said.

"I thought you said you'd sleep," Kozak said.

"I said we'd go on the morn."

"What do you want, Jack. I'm tired."

"I'd ask for a nanodrink if you'd mix for me," Jack said.

"Something to help you sleep at night? What have you done beside springing a convicted criminal?"

"Such crimes as I'd not discuss here and now. No, I'd like Clean Remembrance."

A look of almost pity crossed Kozak's equine features. "Look, there is such a thing as too much remembering. Why don't I give you some Quantum Sound and something to help you appreciate the many ways the day could have gone?"

If the maker wouldn't mix, Jack would make do, walking the dead forest and working over her plans. But better to have the nanodrink. Better if Jack could remember the Court without changing the memories. *CLEAN REMEMBRANCE* allowed this. Yet why should Jack remember a place she was forbidden from ever visiting?

"Seriously, Jack."

"What was your gift, Kozak? What did you will it to be?"

"So, you resort to interrogation? My gift is mine. I'll show you if the time is right. Are you really going to ask me questions all night?"

"Beg pardon. Fare well in sleep."

"You're pitiful. Here. It just took a little while in my pocket lab to mix. Do me a favour and drink it here. Last time I gave you this, you disappeared for three days."

"Was it three?"

"Sit," Kozak said.

Jack took the vial and sat on a knot inside the gazebo. She drank.

The nanodrink didn't make her relive the memories. Jack could talk and think as she always did. But when she hit a thought about the Sixteen Court (as she did now) it would copy that memory in a redundant pattern, find other links to that pattern, and strengthen the pattern so that any remembering she did here and now would reinforce the memories rather than overwrite them.

It only hurt a little.

"So, I won't ask about Huangdi or Ronde again," Kozak said. "But assuming those problems become not-problems, what then? You work for the canine Lifters?"

"It's not so different from the Court, though I'd be alone rather than one of a clan of painters."

Flashes of the impossible walls. When creativity was the only limitation, their structures had grown in sweeps and shapes unbounded. Each flash brought a throb as parts of her memory rewrote.

"I've heard of their hub. It covers a whole planet. It'll be alive and thinking. Can you imagine? A living planet?"

"Is that so strange?" Jack asked.

"Strange? Oh no. I'm just thinking of what I could make with that much space. They should have brought me in to help grow the sentience. Though if Shen Fang was offering, I'm not sure I'd take it."

"You'd speak so of the Lifters?"

"She didn't do the uplifting. Her ancestors did. I respect what they do, but she has her own agenda."

Didn't they all. Jack thought of the Lifters in their visits to the court. Always planning the next species to bring to sentience and equality, seeking the artisans to grow a soul inside the burgeoning mind. The throb was a welcome one.

"Don't get all morose," Kozak said.

"Why don't you have a drink?"

"I have mine alone, thank you. Don't pressure me."

"You're missing out," Jack said.

"Because that isn't messing with you at all, is it?"

Memories throbbed in a rapid pulse that made it hard to reply.

"Go easy, Jack. I'm going to sleep. You stay as long as you want. But don't touch my things."

Jack nodded.

She sat next to the sleeping equine and remembered long into the night.

CHAPTER SIXTEEN

The gift demon fled.

She took her giantess body through one-door after one-door, watching the chaos hide her with a kind of glee.

Where disasters happened and untimely deaths of the young, where injuries that shouldn't have occurred did, and where the weather took a turn for the worse, trapping travellers in caves to freeze and starve; there she passed unseen. Tragedy was her cloak and injury her cowl. None saw through her screen of pain.

None but the artists, of course, and now two of them hunted her.

The gift demon used the seeking stones and travelled to another place. She hid in a world that moved on. Maybe here she'd be beyond the painter and the bard.

--•--

As the white dwarf sun rose above the horizon, Jack opened the canvas and began painting a portal. Her companions stood ready.

Rosahu, Uma Kozak, you have no obligation to carry on with us, Wolfgang said.

"You mean we don't have crazy oaths we've sworn," Kozak

said. "I'm not in a hurry to get home after my recent public appearances."

As you say, Uma Kozak, Wolfgang said.

Rosahu shifted between male and fem. She pointed to her own chest, then to Jack. "I'm w ... w-with you."

The crystal brush and painting surface didn't buck so much today. Or maybe Jack was getting reacquainted with such power again.

"Where are you taking us, young paintslinger?" Shen Fang asked. "Do you so easily travel to the gift demon?"

Wolfgang kindly answered. *A wise question, Lifter. Jack is taking us to a one-door, a place with limited connectedness to other worlds. One opening going to one place at a time, sometimes only one place ever. Or one time ever. The gift demon favours such places to hide and to travel.*

"The gift demon likes a kind of place," Jack said. She painted the war-torn mountainside leading to ancient stones of primitive magic, she'd seen in other realities. "The gift demon has already used this place or will use it. It comes with the kind of pain she savours."

As Jack moved to depict the seeking stones, their circular pattern of spheres with a larger central orb, the canvas thrummed and pushed against her strokes. Old magic. Older than the Sixteen Court and alive in different ways. Yet, all magic could be depicted under the hands of a skilful artist. Or perhaps one that had been around for a few years, anyway.

"Danger?" Rosahu asked.

"Tel-man, how long have you been with us now?" Kozak said. "Of course, there is danger."

Rosahu nodded and grew muscle and height.

Jack added to the depiction, until she could remove the painting plane and leave the hole in air.

Clouds drifted below the mountainside. Ancient markers

stood in formations of honour along a winding stone staircase up to the circle. On a flat terraced section of the giant mountain, hidden except to those as knew of it, the perfectly spherical seeking stones stood proud from ground and—to those with artists eyes—from reality itself. Sparse mountain trees with vines dotted the landscape, and caves made dark spaces in the rocky slope.

An idea occurred to Jack. If the gift demon had indeed been here ...

Jack added the remains of a rockslide pressing up against the circle formation. A crashed elemental zeppelin lay crumpled against one side of the mountain, and a lava spurt started a fire along the higher foliage. A shame to mar such beauty with chaos, but such chaos was honesty with the gift demon.

In this world, the air of the forest flowed into the portal, and eddies of mountain breeze touched Jack's nose.

"Good enough, Jack," Kozak said.

Jack added a flourish of cloth flapping on the zeppelin's frame and nodded. She stepped through onto the winding stairs.

The others came after. Rosahu and Wolfgang moved off the path immediately, gripping the rugged trees of mountain heights. Shen Fang stood beside Jack and breathed the air with closed eyes.

"Stairs. What is it with bipeds and stairs?" Kozak said. "It's lazy design."

"What would you prefer?" Jack asked.

"I'll show you some designs I came up with for a mountain world recently. Adaptive footpaths. Not just stupid terraces spaced uniformly for bipeds."

"Hmm, should we leave this portal open?" Shen Fang asked.

PAINTSLINGER

Through the portal, the stone banyan trees seemed to wane in the light. Such beauty, ended by Wylan without a moment's thought.

"As you say," Jack said. She painted the hole gone in a few strokes of sky. "Rosahu, Wolfgang, don't attack what you see."

They gestured agreement, and all climbed upward. The thin air made steps harder and talk was sparse, until Wolfgang gestured that there was movement ahead in a copse.

Jack found a vial in one of her buttoned pockets and drank.

The copse of trees straggled over the lip of the flat where the spheres stood. With thermal vision slowly augmenting her sight, Jack saw the warm spot in the thick tangle of the tree boughs.

It looked like a shark from water-worlds, only quadruped with webbed skin between the limbs and a bearing a fur coating. It was larger than Wolfgang.

It watched them back.

"There is a watcher above," Jack said. "A creature of this world."

"Sentient?" Kozak asked.

Jack borrowed Rosahu's gesture, a seesaw of the hand.

Shall I engage? Wolfgang wrote.

"No. It's the distraction," Jack said.

"From what?" Shen Fang asked.

"The other danger."

Jack hadn't been sure when she depicted this place, but the seeking stones sometimes had guardians or protectors. If so, the guardian must have come from a powerful circle to be so far away.

"Peace," Jack called. She raised her arms, and her canvas folded and settled in its place on the back of her hand.

No answer.

"We know of your mistress's nature magic," Jack said, "and we seek the aid of her followers. We would ask for your aid in bearing the weight of our knowledge, though we will not be able to carry yours."

The thin rocks slid away to the right, and a hunter stood in rugged leathers. He wore two curved blades on his hips. He looked cold to Jack's thermal vision, until he stood. Jack hadn't seen him, though now that he was on his feet, pockets of heat bloomed on his skin.

"Peace to you also," he called, hands raised in kind. "I dreamt of a traveller with sharp eyes. You must have sharp eyes to see Sato when she does not want to be seen."

"You are kind. Your sharp-eyed traveller may yet come if you hold fast. May we confer in the open?" she asked.

"Off the stairs, please," Kozak added.

"I didn't build them. We don't build stairs to our stones." The hunter looked to Jack. "You must have a strong bond with her. She takes speech from you?" He gestured to Kozak.

"If anything, I get speech from her. Would you give us aid and counsel?"

He nodded and loped up the scree to a cave. He seemed too thin to be so strong. He reminded Jack of warrior shamans in some of the tribal cultures. To his credit, when they sat inside the arch of a large enough cave, he didn't respond aversely to the varied shapes of the people he met. Though if Shen Fang spoke aloud, he might make more comments about the bond.

The shark creature joined them and sat close to the hunter.

"You may call me Marau. Myself and Sato are pleased to have you. This is why you still live," Marau said. "That and because I dreamt of your visit. You seek death."

"Of a sort. I'm Jack. This is Shen Fang, Rosahu, and Wolfgang. And she's Kozak. The death I seek came this way and used the seeking stones."

Marau looked at the cave roof as though seeing through to the spheres above. "You name them oddly, and I would not speak of such things."

You should tell him you are a guardian like him, Wolfgang said.

"She speaks to me with her script?" Marau said.

"Wolfgang does at that. She'd have you know our goals are similar. I painted—I mean I saw some crashed flying machinery."

"Aye, the zeppelin came and caused the rockslide. Whether it also caused the mountain's heart to become active and erupt, I do not know. I was asleep."

"In your sleep, did you see anything unusual?" Jack asked.

"Who sees in their sleep, traveller?" Marau asked.

"In sleep, none. Though some would watch in nature's realm," Jack said. It was a gamble to speak of such things. In neighbouring worlds, there were those that saw in a mirror world while sleeping, though Jack didn't know if they used spark or spell. They dressed like Marau. Unless she was mistaken about his origins.

Marau looked at each of them in turn before settling his gaze back on Jack. "You speak freely with secrets that are not yours."

"Beg pardon, I once knew someone who spoke like you. She was kind to me in time of need. I am too familiar since then."

"Sato wants to know what you mean when you say 'unusual,'" Marau said.

"A shadow unlike the haunter's of nature's realm," Jack said. "A movement that made blades of grass all point one way, and that way being a way that made you uncomfortable to see. Bad shapes in the random arrangements of stone or leaf. Some would fear such shadows, and some would try to fight it. Did you try to hunt it in the dream realm?"

"Sato would not speak of her hunt that night. We were favoured to escape the dangers that arose."

"I believe a gift demon passed that night and used the seeking stones to travel to another one-door."

"The stones can tell me. If you lie, we will do battle, and I will kill you all. To lie of the stones, one can mean naught but ill." Marau stood. "I will go now. Sato wants me to spare you, but even Sato will attack if you move with deceit while I go. Do you agree?"

"By my court and my oaths, I agree," Jack said with a slight bow.

Marau lingered at that. He considered something, though what he weighed was a mystery. Then he walked out of the cave and began the climb the rest of the way to the spheres on the mountainside above.

Sato's mouth opened and closed in a yawn, showing rows of razor teeth.

"Thanks for speaking for all of us, Jack," Kozak said.

"I thought Jack was rather kind to the man considering the threats," Shen Fang said. "A lesser person might have been piqued!"

"He's a long way from home," Jack said. "Violence is the safer way on this world. I'd not let him harm us, should he try. Nor would I let you, Sato. You aren't from here. Strange to see the hunter bond with someone on a different world. You cared for him when he was lost?"

Sato paused, then reached with webbed forelimb and drew symbols in the dust of the cave floor, erasing then drawing again.

Wolfgang read and wrote in her own calligraphy. *The human would have perished. Sato took pity when he appeared among the spheres with the remains of his companion. At first the human refused her aid. The words she uses don't exactly mean aid. Something more along the lines of mercy or rescue. Sato is part of a predator group here. They do not spare often.*

"You understand Common," Jack said.

Again, Sato wrote, but before Wolfgang could translate, Marau dropped into the cave.

Jack let her hand rest beside her brushes.

"Death seeker," Marau said. "Your words are truth." He looked over his shoulder. He was afraid of something?

Sato rose on massive haunches and moved to the edge of the cave. Marau put his hand on Sato's side and said, "I'm sorry."

Sato dove out of the cave.

"What is it?" Shen Fang asked.

"Someone attacks her people in the valley," Marua said. "They bring magic that turns life to stone, and the stone soldiers among them still move. Has my war reached so far to come here?"

Jack stood. "Perhaps, though I believe I know this enemy. Her name is Wylan Ronde. She is lazy, but dangerous."

"I must help Sato," Marau said.

If Jack let him go to Sato's aid, he wouldn't be able to send them through the spheres, the seeking stones. "Wait," Jack said. "If one of us goes and helps now, would you send the rest of us through?"

"Which of you would fight with her?" Marau asked. He seemed ready to refuse if Jack offered the wrong person.

Jack looked to Wolfgang. She gestured with her forelimb and rose to her full height. She unsheathed her blade.

Marau nodded. "Please. Be strong with her."

My blade and my brush are hers. With that, Wolfgang ran out of the cave.

"So Marau, you're staying to help us instead of going to

your friend?" Kozak said. "I mean, it's great and all, but you don't know us."

"Aye, though you misunderstand. Come," Marau said. He climbed out of the cave.

Jack, Shen Fang, Kozak and Rosahu followed back onto the scree and up the side of the mountain.

"I am forbidden by Sato to leave this place," Marau said as he climbed. "Sato's sisters and brothers did not welcome the stones. Those who came before were not humble. Others have come through and settled in this world. They too were immodest."

"Does Sato eat people when they are immodest?" Kozak asked.

"They may save them and rear them for eating later," Marau said. "Sato should not have spared me. She is a thief to her kind, though even a thief would be treated kindlier than me."

"So you'd go and fight for Sato and the furry shark people, even though they'd save you for a festival meal?" Kozak asked.

"Yes, though you all helped me keep my promise to Sato in sending your friend to help. Your ally seems a strong warrior."

"So she is," Jack said. "You'll help her come through after the battle?"

"If she lives, I will send her," Marau said. He reached the ledge where the spheres lay. He pulled himself onto it.

"I thank you," Jack said. The last ledge proved difficult to scale. Rosahu went first and helped Jack. Shen Fang seemed almost to glide up. Kozak took a different route.

Lichen and moss stained the smaller stones that made the outer ring. They stood taller even than Rosahu in her current shape. The centre sphere seemed too smooth for something of this size, double that of the smaller spheres. Its bottom kissed the ground. No depression or ditch marred the earth beneath it, as though the centre sphere wasn't wholly in this world, which of course it wasn't.

Kozak trotted into the circle arrangement from the rockslide at the back. "I had to go above it and come down. How does this work? Are these spheres sentient?"

"Please," Marau gestured for them to touch the sphere at the heart of the circle.

"Secrets, right," Kozak said.

"Where are you sending us?" Jack asked.

"The death you seek went into a shadow world. Not another realm, and not a physical place. I do not understand its location or its nature."

That could mean any number of things.

Marau looked back. Clouds drifted over the battle below.

"Wolfgang will help her," Jack said. And if Jack felt a pang of worry for her friend, it would do nothing to share it.

The hunter turned back to the stones. "I believe you. If you see when you travel, touch nothing. Not all life in the space between is good."

Jack nodded. He wasn't wrong.

"Farewell," he said. He closed his eyes, and the air in front of his chest began to glow green.

A flash, then, and they disappeared among the stones.

CHAPTER SEVENTEEN

The gift demon moved to leave the simulated reality.

Elsewhere in the sim, computer memory failed. People and places were erased. Glitches maimed the innocent, and experiences were lost to corruption.

Should either of the artists follow, they risked erasure in the simulation.

So it was that she left this reality unnoticed, dematerialising unseen in the fictitious cave. The bipeds scurried to repair themselves as the gift demon moved from the sim into this reality's 'real' world.

--•--

A flash of green shone bright on a mountainside near stone spheres, and a battle played out below. In the valley, Wylan strolled into the town with her lute in hand and her stone golems before her. The gift demon had come this way, and she had her orders.

Nearby, a wall collapsed, human prisoners appeared, fattened and stumpy of arm and leg. One of them stopped in front of her.

"Thank you! Now run! Get away!" He kept ranting as he turned and fled through warrens behind Wylan.

PAINTSLINGER

In that moment, could it be, Wylan felt ... good? From accidentally helping someone? Better not to dwell on such thoughts. Moral high grounds were made of sand.

So as the stone soldiers guarded her in a shield wall from the furry shark things, Wylan moved. A rushing stance, weight on bent front leg, and she rotated her hips and spine as she brought the lute vertical in front of her, shifting the weight from the front leg to the back. She lifted her forward foot and let the heel touch the ground, toe up. Standing so, she breathed, gripping the neck of the vertical lute with her front hand, strings to the side, and with her back hand, she strummed in a forward motion. A discordant wisp flew from the lute at the speed of sound, cutting the webbed limb of a shark thing ahead. It stumbled and fell, bleeding.

Step, and again. With each strum, Wylan played a song of death, notes flying like barbs, barely visible as blurs and striking the giant shark things. They looked like crosses between giant frogs and furry sharks, but they fought like crazy.

Fun. Not because Wylan had helped anyone, of course. Letting loose on primitives with the lute forms just felt good.

Another thought clashed in her mind. If she wasn't helping anyone, why had she kept so much of the stone army back? Was it to prevent the magic of the dragon from turning this world to stone, too?

Maybe, but for selfish reasons. Always for selfish reasons. Altruism was the greatest lie told by the Sixteen Court.

The green light that had flickered before on the mountaintop now flared, solar bright, and Wylan winced.

Jack? Was she chasing the gift demon, too?

Wylan forced herself to resume the song on her lute. Not a problem. If Jack focused on the gift demon and the gift demon focused on Jack, Wylan's job of chasing the gift demon away was that much easier.

Wylan strummed, killing a creature, and moved on, and as the people spilled out from cages and cells, Wylan ignored them, or tried anyway.

--•--

A green flash, and Jack saw in the space between worlds and time.

Her own shape kept changing, growing and shrinking, as though she could see a portion of the time-vine version of herself, the four-dimensional being that made up the summation of her choices and history. The cross-section of who she was now, and now, and now again grew and shrank. The thought reminded her of the lysts, predators of time, that saw this way.

The spheres grew and shrank likewise. They pinched and flickered as though Jack saw single pearls in a string necklace and somehow travelled via them.

A shadow moved outside the spheres, a huge thing forever away, cosmic distances away. So for the shadow to be visibly moving, it had to be reaching relativistic speeds. It made her mind hurt like thin places.

Jack created imbalance when she brought order from chaos. There were days when Jack thought some of the things outside the realities had taken notice. So yes. As Marau had said: not all life in the space between was good.

Brightness grew and then black.

--•--

Noise came of dripping water. It echoed as against stone. Each echo sounded exactly like the last. Pitch perfect exact.

As Jack's eyes adjusted, shapes became visible. Stalactites

above, and fire light flickered from a nearby cave into this one. Each flicker had a pattern. Dim, dim, bright, dim, repeat.

"It's a sim," Kozak said, appearing next to Jack. "That's what the human meant when he said a shadow world, isn't it?"

"Yes," Jack agreed. "It's definitely a spark world."

Kozak, Rosahu, Shen Fang, all present. Good. Wolfgang would be along shortly. No need to worry there. She was fully grown and completely capable.

"She'll be fine," Kozak said.

"Who?" Jack asked with a shrug.

Shen Fang patted Jack on the shoulder.

Footsteps splashed in the tunnel. Each splash sounded identical.

And then one didn't sound identical. It sounded stretched and slow, and in the slowness, it had a broken stepped quality. A person cried out.

Jack walked into the tunnel to find a two people, one sitting and one standing. They had lowered masks and large satchels thrown over their shoulders.

"Easy. I'm Jack."

"And what are they?" The one standing asked. She turned, seeming ready to run.

"Friends," Jack said.

"Okay friends. I'm Daphnea. And this is totally my bag. I own it and everything in it. Also, can you help me with him?"

"Who is he?"

"My ... friend also. Yes. We are friends. He is Jame and we are friends and we are supposed to be here. The world is flickering and weird, and he fell. I should go, shouldn't I? I'll go."

Kozak looked to Jack. Jack shook her head. These people might not know they were in a spark world. And Daphnea seemed in a hurry to get away.

Jame's eyes rolled back in his head and he slumped against the wet rock wall.

"Oh hell," she said. "Now I'm never going to get paid."

"Say, we could help your friend if you guide us?" Shen Fang said.

"The dog talks. Right." She faced Kozak. "I guess I shouldn't ask you to carry my bag, then?"

"Rude," Kozak said.

"Cry pardon," Jack cut in. Jack needed to catch the gift demon, and these had their own ends in mind. "We'll let you be on your way."

"Wait. He owes me a large sum of money. Help me haul him and I'll see if I can return the favour?"

There wasn't time for this, but she might know of the gift demon and the path of destruction. Or more likely lead Jack to someone who could help.

Jack bent and lifted his arm around her shoulder. Daphnea did the same and they lifted. They walked with his weight between them.

Oddly, Jack had to strain under his weight. Odd to see a limitation in a simulation. She looked to Kozak, who seemed to be taking everything in, measuring every detail: sound, light, and weight in her mind. Good. Hopefully Kozak would puzzle out the rules of this place. Jack had no love of spark worlds.

Each junction and tunnel branch looked identical until they came to a heavy metal door. Daphnea looked both ways in the tunnel before placing her hand on the metal. The brushed metal dissolved under her touch, revealing a doorway to a room of tile, stainless steel, and artificial lights. An infirmary of sorts?

With some awkward effort, Jame went onto a table, laid down. Jack breathed and checked her pack. It seemed wise with present company.

Instruments appeared at either side, and cables materialised onto his body. Daphnea tapped the instruments.

Kozak moved close to Jack and spoke in a low voice. "They can modify the sim from within the sim. It's a dangerous setup for any sentient inhabitants."

Loud enough for Daphnea to hear, Kozak said, "I might be able to help."

"Thank goodness. This is not my thing. Our spell medic—is fine! One hundred percent fine, yet also unavailable."

"I'm something of a ... spell master. Or something," Kozak gestured with her right prosthetic arm, and a control panel appeared floating in air. She gestured again, and it vanished.

"You? Really?" Daphnea said.

"You really don't want to get paid, do you?" Kozak said.

A pause.

"Daphnea?" Jack asked.

"I'm thinking." Daphnea said. "Okay, yes. You help us and we'll be on our way."

"So what happened to him?" Kozak asked while tapping the panel beside the table.

"All of Haven has things appearing, disappearing for a couple sleep cycles, right? Everyone's distracted. We were working, Jame and I, legitimately working at our real and true jobs outside that storage vault, and he stepped and the water became ice. He hit his head when he fell, threw up, and that's when you came."

Kozak kept tapping, panels materialising and disappearing as she moved her two main prosthetic arms. Her third arm tapped her muscled neck in what Jack always assumed was an act of concentration.

"Is there a path to the strangeness?" Jack asked.

"Maybe." Daphnea said. "It definitely started near the storage vault. Then it hit the market. Walls move, people crumple over dead or just vanish, and the market stalls claim to be out of my favourite ale, though we'll see about that."

Now the panels showed symbols of text rather than pictures or mechanical switches. Kozak moved directly through the code, scanning lines, flipping to a new panel, and doing the same. Which was great, but every moment they were here, the gift demon got further away.

Jame's eyes opened and the cables vanished.

"Hello?" He said.

"Easy," Jack said.

"I didn't do it! Daphnea—"

"—is right here." Daphnea said.

He caught sight of her and felt his shirt pockets.

"Hand it over," he said.

"Your passkey got lost, sadly." Daphnea said.

"Then so did your payday. How did you help me anyway? Our spell medic—"

"—is still fine, as I'm sure you remember! Oh, here's the passkey after all." She rummaged in her satchel and handed a white keycard to him. These people and animals are friends, Jame. So let's say thanks and we'll just be on our way. Thanks so much!" Daphnea said.

Jack cleared her throat. "I'm sure you can answer some questions before you go."

They exchanged a glance as Jame got off the table.

Kozak sighed. "Maybe your world has rewards or something?"

"Kozak," Jack said.

"I'm just reading the room," Kozak said.

"You raise a valid point. Haven needs our help." Daphnea said. "You can do more of your spell casting, right? What can I do for you?"

PAINTSLINGER

"First," Jack said, "a companion should be following us shortly. Will we know when she comes?"

"The only way into Haven is the way you came. The way out is on the other side of the cave system. No one ever comes, though. At least not people as, diverse, shall we say, as you? But all tunnels eventually lead to the market, and from there your friend should find her way. What is your friend, anyway? A talking fish?"

"Arachnid," Kozak said.

"Cool." Daphnea said.

"Secondly," Jack said, "the harm you see here is happening elsewhere right now. I aim to stop that harm. All you need to do is show me the way out and resume your trade craft."

"Sounds splendid." Daphnea said. "After your spell caster—Kozak, right—after Kozak helps us?"

One metal wall flickered and disappeared. Rock showed where the wall had been.

"Kozak, can you cast from anywhere?" Jack asked.

"Not yet," Kozak said. "This room has special rules. But ..."

She gestured, scrolled through code, scrolled some more.

"Kozak," Jack asked.

"Two seconds," Kozak said. She materialised three new prosthetic limbs floating beside her and those were typing, too. And again. Nine limbs typing.

Another wall disappeared. Pebbles fell from the ceiling where the wall had been.

"I don't mean to rush you," Jack said.

"Good. Don't, then. I'm almost there," Kozak said. "Actually, I am there," Kozak tapped loudly, and the walls reappeared.

"You can make changes anywhere now?" Jack asked.

"Kind of. I can control these lovely new limbs. And they can stay here. I tried to find the location-based limitations, but someone kept rushing me."

"Beg your pardon," Jack said. "Daphnea, lead the way."

Daphnea looked to Kozak. "And you'll help with that reward? Also, could this work with locked doors?"

"Whatever. Should be pretty easy to arrange something now that I've got control."

Daphnea nodded and gestured to follow.

As they walked, Kozak would call a panel and tap it, solidifying a wall or restoring a flickering flame.

"Why Haven?" Rosahu asked.

"Why do we call it that?" Daphnea asked.

Rosahu nodded.

Jack tried to listen, focusing on this place rather than the gift demon's wake. Or on the dubious activities of these would-be helpers.

"My great grandparents lived in the badlands. Lots of fighting and disease, right? So, the spell casters created Haven. They made a place to go where people had ways to live and wouldn't fight any more. They say some people stayed in the badlands, maintaining the spells, but the fighting made it hard to breathe or see without getting sick. So, they changed Haven to allow spells on the inside."

The tunnel widened, and artificial light mixed with firelight. A din of voices and activity rose, and Jack stepped into a huge cavern. Stairs led down to a floor area a kilometre across where a market appeared to be set up. People rushed between stalls and tents. Everything flickered.

"Oh hell," Kozak said.

"Bad?" Jack asked.

"No," Kozak said, "but it's a lot. Not just one thing went wrong. Storage failed, crosstalk and lost data, power surges. You name it. I've been repairing as I can but this is crazy. Jack, this is going to take time."

"I'm afraid we need your help, too, maker," Jack said.

PAINTSLINGER

Kozak gestured, a wave of prosthetic arm over the damage happening everywhere. Stalactites fell on tent stalls. Fires erupted, and people flickered in and out of existing, falling and crying out.

Shen Fang put a paw on Jack's shoulder.

Kozak brought up panels and began typing.

"She c ... c-an help," Rosahu said.

Which Jack knew. That wasn't the problem. The problem was the gift demon, who had done all this before. Jack had set out with twenty people last time, and in the end, only she made it to the gift demon.

"When Wolfgang comes through, you come with her, okay?" Jack said.

"Don't worry, paintslinger," Kozak said. "True, I've never done this before. But I'm very, very good."

"That you are, maker. I'd ask you join me again. This time without a death sentence getting in the way."

Kozak nodded. "Daphnea, where is your nearest med bay? I'll set up more remotes."

Daphnea pointed down the stairs, along the cave wall toward a tunnel on the lower level.

Kozak left them, setting off mumbling about bipeds and stairs as she went.

"How do we get to the badlands?" Jack asked.

"I will get paid, won't I?" Daphnea asked.

Jack nodded.

"Okay. Follow me," Daphnea said.

Jack followed on a scaffold path around the huge market cave to a tunnel that led down.

As she walked on the incline, Jack thought of a debate she might have with Kozak when she caught up. Generations were possible inside, which meant reproduction and ageing. Were these offspring technically spark golems—or artificial intelligence as Kozak might put it—since they had no physical history?

A good question for Kozak when she followed. Not that Jack was worried. Kozak would catch up with Wolfgang in no time.

A wind blew up the tunnel. It smelled acrid.

"What's that smell?" Jack asked.

"That's the door," Daphnea said.

Ahead the tunnel bent. It was too long, somehow, curving at an angle to the right that it shouldn't have been able to turn. Shadows shifted from the lights, but the shadows didn't seem to match the shapes in the tunnel.

"The door to the badlands is a little weird. Just keep walking," Daphnea said.

Shen Fang smiled. "You are kind to travellers! I would like to see you again. Would it be okay if I came back?"

Daphnea shrugged and turned.

"Farewell, Daphnea," Jack said. "Thank you for your kindness."

Daphnea paused. "Out of curiosity, are you really a paintslinger?" Daphnea asked. "Kozak called you one. I've heard of paintslinger knights." She clutched her satchel tighter as she asked.

Jack paused, then thought of Wylan, and what she might do if she came to this place.

"I'm a traveller like any other," Jack lied.

Daphnea nodded, relaxing in her shoulders.

"You might be more careful in your legitimate work," Jack said. "Or perhaps abandon it for safer endeavours?"

"Sorry? The sound is not great in this part of the tunnel. Anyway, good luck!"

She walked away leaving Jack, Shen Fang, and Rosahu.

Jack turned, walked, and after a few steps, vanished.

PAINTSLINGER

And appeared in some kind of fluid.

-•-

Jack swam toward light and broke the surface of the fluid, breathing tentatively at first and then readily.

Saltwater came away as Jack pulled herself out of a vat.

The giant tub stood in an ancient warehouse, part of some machination that no longer functioned. The hum of a generator echoed through the dusty place and bars of light shone through the slatted roof overhead.

The engine hum seemed to have a melody to it. A whisper that almost had meaning, words and shapes.

Jack shook her head and dripping, knelt on the walkway beside the vat.

Rosahu surfaced, then Shen Fang. Jack helped Rosahu out. Shen Fang ascended, pulling one handed to rise above the saltwater and gliding to the wood of the walkway.

Then they saw the bodies.

Stone golems lay shattered all over the dusty warehouse floor. Jack looked at the vat they had come out of. It was one of three, but the golems hadn't come by the vats. They had been trying to get in.

"Tread lightly," Jack said.

"Traps?" Rosahu asked.

"I'd guess so," Jack said. "The spark world we just left has lasted many generations. It wouldn't have survived without a means of protecting itself. Hopefully, they are clever enough to know we are coming out rather than going in."

Jack found the old cement stairs and walked down to the main floor.

"This is worse than I thought," Shen Fang said. "The dragon in the man mask has attacked this world already."

Jack considered arguing with her but left it. It did seem odd that Wylan had been in the mountain world with the furred sharks, and yet these stone golems were here. Odd ... unless Huangdi really was behind the assaults?

Well. Even so, Jack needed the gift demon to fulfil her promise. Jack needed unlimited paint to help the canines.

In the strewn stone and dust, which way had the gift demon gone? There wasn't a path of chaos here. The whole factory floor was chaos.

Jack lifted her bandanna and lowered her goggles and walked among the shattered golems. The nearest exit was a double door, ten metres high and fifteen wide, split down the middle by a hinge to open both ways. Meant for loading and unloading in the time before.

Jack pushed, and the doors screeched open against rust.

Outside the sun was tired, and the dust swirled free of brush or bramble. The hum was louder. A thin place. Jack tried not to hear its whispers. Doors often had whispers, but Jack intended on taking many more doors in her time. Listening to one was a good way to end travel forever.

A field of golems outside lay unmoving, baking and dust blown.

All but one. One shifted. No legs and only one arm, but it tried to drag itself with its arm.

Jack circled the golem and knelt where it could see her, and she it. Fine sculpting, but old, in harsh chisels that had been stylish in an age before. Not likely Wylan's work but familiar.

"Hail," Jack said.

It stopped its one-armed crawl and watched her.

"You seek to return to your master?" Jack asked the golem. "You may answer freely. We have no fight at present."

It nodded.

Yes, the texture of the armour was something Jack had

seen sculpted by some of the best in the world. Definitely not Wylan. It had a flair that Jack had mimicked in her own depictions. And did it hurt to see it so? To see familiarity in the bearing of an enemy? Some thought such were the only true injuries.

"Is Wylan Ronde your master?" she asked, already knowing the answer.

The golem's mouth opened, and it coughed the dead air of tombs.

No. Not coughed. Laughed.

"If I see your kind again in the act of crimes, I will bring judgement to the maker. Tell your master so. There will be no bargains."

The one-armed drag continued, and the golem coughed its cavern laugh.

And Jack realised what she'd heard a moment earlier. Shen Fang had a clumsy moment?

Jack stood and dusted herself off. She left the laughing stone golem and went back inside the old building.

"Auntie," Jack said. "We need to—"

"Ow," Shen Fang said, tripping as she walked. "A clumsy moment. Don't worry, I only stumbled! I'm okay!"

"Auntie, freeze." Jack signalled to Rosahu and stepped over rubble to stand beside Shen Fang.

She pointed to a hatch in the floor. "I didn't see the handle."

Except Shen Fang had the grace of a dancer and a fighter in one. Shen Fang saw everything. Clumsiness could happen but ...

Jack walked to the hatch and pulled the handle.

The rusted bar broke free.

Unlucky.

Jack tried to wedge the bar underneath the hatch.

Her boot heel came loose, and she slipped.

"The gift demon went this way," Jack said.

Rosahu grew herself larger and more muscular, joints popping, then pushed the hatch down until it bucked and the edge had a lip that could be grabbed.

"Thank you, singer," Jack said.

Rosahu nodded and pulled the hatch open.

Jack climbed down first.

CHAPTER EIGHTEEN

Back in the furry shark world, sweat poured from Wylan's skin.

Where had the stupid spider come from?

A ward flew from Wolfgang, amber and hot with scents of honey. Wylan dodged and strummed, fanning the strings as fast as she could while backing away. Discordant thrums flew. Wolfgang deflected these with sword and ward.

Was Wylan worried? Certainly not.

The stone feline fought beside Wylan, slashing claws and leaping around like a circus acrobat, mostly handling the furry shark things, until Wolfgang leapt above the fray and landed next to the cat.

Wylan raked the strings hard, each note a thrown barb, and one struck Wolfgang's sword limb.

Wolfgang stumbled, her sword falling free of her grip.

While the cat leapt out of danger, Wylan sealed the deal. She took in this moment, this victory, and sent a chord of hot slices, cutting clean through Wolfgang's sword limb. The severed appendage dropped. Wolfgang visibly shivered with pain.

A second chord prepared, but Wolfgang moved faster, creating her own ward. The spider's jade brush slashed, bright purple shot forward and hit the lute in Wylan's hand. The lute twanged and burst and fell from her grasp.

Never mind this. Fighting here was a waste of time. Especially when the stone golems could finish off the spider. Better to use tools than to get one's own hands dirty. Besides, Wylan had places to go and gift demons to hunt.

The golems surrounded Wolfgang, pulling the spider's focus. Wylan turned to the cat. "I think it's time for your travel skills, my furry friend."

The feline didn't obey. It wasn't stone any more. It must have been the distance from the dragon emperor. This was a problem. Hopefully, the feline wouldn't do anything stupid. It would be a pity to destroy such a useful vehicle.

How else would she travel?

Speaking of, time really was growing short.

And the wounded spider still fended off the golems, faring quite well without her sword. Wards ripped through one stone golem, scattering crushed stone. Another filled the gap. But supplies were not endless.

"Hey, you. You crazy cat. Shall we get out of here and settle whatever disagreement we have?"

"You mean to betray the dragon in the man mask," the feline said.

She wanted to talk. Now? Not the best timing in the midst of a battle, but Wylan was always up for a chat as long as the stone golems did their thing. And so long as the chat was brief. Not that she was worried, of course.

For privacy's sake, Wylan used her brush to cast an illusion ward. If the spider made it through the golems and looked this way, it would appear as though she and the cat had vanished in smoke. She couldn't have the arachnid following her, could she?

"Old pal," Wylan said. "The man emperor wants to die. Is it betrayal to help with that goal? Now. If the man emperor changes his mind, I might have to respect his earlier intentions. Do you get me?"

"You almost got me killed," she said.

"Listen. Um, what's your name again?"

"Asami," she said.

"Asami, right. Sorry, today's been crazy. Anyway, you could say I almost got you killed. Or you could remember how much *fun* it all was. You've seen the cosmos with me. Your kind can always travel, but I showed you where to go, didn't I? I gave you a thrill."

She paused at that. Then she said, "If I help you, the raids will stop?" Yes, there was something else in that pause. Sure, Asami wanted her home to stop being raided. Fine. But she'd also taken a liking to their little path.

Wylan put her arm around Asami's shoulders. "Friend, the raids only stop if we kill the man emperor. After that, the new leader can do whatever she wants. Would you like this incredibly capable benefactor to protect your home?"

"Just leave it alone," Asami said.

"Sure, fine, great. Now, I don't mean to rush, but we've got some enemies here." Wylan said, gesturing to the spider who was blasting wards through the last of the golems. Seconds. They had seconds. Not that she was worried, of course, but ... priorities. "Can we, you know, do your little travel thing?"

Asami nodded. "There's a forest further down the mountain. A tree there exists in other worlds, too. Bardo worlds."

Wylan clapped. "Lead the way, you."

"Asami," she said.

"Right. Lead the way, Asami."

She did. And in good time. Behind them, the last of the golems dropped at the spider's casting. Could spiders seethe? All eight of those eyes looked as though they could, all wide-open and gaping.

But the spider was stuck here now, standing on her seven

remaining legs with nothing but her impotent rage to pass the time.

How marvellous!

She waved her fingers at the arachnid as the cat took her toward her prize.

−•−

The gift demon crossed time. Artists dreaded to go so far, yet the chaos that hid the demon also allowed time its continuity. No paradoxes rose from the kind of pain she caused. Some even thought her wake preserved time.

She travelled by thin place to a planet that the inhabitants called Earth. How quaint. She stopped on an island someone had named the United Kingdom. Demons could pass through such a place in its primitive time without notice. The year was 2016 ACE in the old earth calendar, where and when the people had become too absorbed with their own business to see the struggles of their own kind.

In the dark hours of an early day, the gift demon prowled through a narrow street in a Surrey city. Crowded homes lined cramped roads, alongside offices and shops.

This would do.

She stopped in one suburban street in front of a three story Victorian-style home. An accountant with a class status of Knight who had never defended anyone lost his keys. Lovely, yes, this could compound well. A few streets over, outside a pawnbroker's shop, a mobility scooter battery died in the freezing rain, leaving the handicapped girl two miles from home. Her cold frustration reached the demon like a perfume. Between the Victorian home and the broken-down scooter, a transformer at the top of a wooden pole blew. City power went down for a mile. Within that mile, a shopping centre selling clothes and phones went dark. Sleeping in the overhang of the department store, a homeless man in a sleeping bag felt his cough become fluidic. A fox leapt warily away from the cough and rushed across the cobbled road. And on the other side of town, all the traffic lights at an intersection turned green at the same time. A builder in his truck with his tools drove full-speed ahead, as a boy walked into the road.

Yes. This would do quite nicely, indeed.

Let artists come here.

Let them behold her wake.

–•–

Shen Fang said, "Wait."

In the tunnel, Jack held a paint light above a painted glove as before. This had been a maintenance area for Haven, but something was wrong.

"Auntie?" Jack said.

"Do you know how we are building a world hub?" Shen Fang said.

"As in, the method you use? Spark or spell?"

Shen Fang shook her head. "It is not usually spoken of, but canines generally have greater ability to detect things than other species. Things and places."

Was Shen Fang being coy? Or was she truly worried about something?

Either worried Jack.

"Thin places?" Rosahu asked.

Gift demons didn't travel by thin places. No one did. People stumbled into them and disappeared, or they escaped, but they didn't go through them. Dead bardo worlds lay between, wastes and ruins and cosmic collapses. Only gap crossers moved freely, and even they shied away when the gaze of one of the things outside reality fell across one of the dead bardo worlds.

Jack ducked under a low pipe and held her goggles to her head. "Pardon, Auntie, but thin places can't be turned into a world hub."

Shen Fang held aside a bundle of cables for Jack and gestured. "And that, paintslinger, is why there are no more world hubs. That's why even the knowledge of them is lost. The last one was built with the help of the Sixteen Court. Before your time. Four knights, the number of death, went into the dead bardo worlds for us. They never returned, but they secured the worlds that allowed us to connect realities."

Yes, before Jack's time there had been knights who had journeyed and never returned. But four together? And what could destroy not one but four paintslinger knights?

There were times, like now, that Jack didn't so much care for being the last of her kind. If four knights couldn't survive the thin places, how could she?

Jack stopped in the abandoned metal corridor.

"I see your worry. We aren't asking you to do the same. Only the bard needs dealing with."

Yes. Well. Layers of truth and all that.

"You mean for us to follow the gift demon through a thin place. If I use the canvas and paint before we find the gift demon, while we are in the dead bardo worlds, I might run out."

"It will not come to that," Shen Fang said. "Remember the gift demon doesn't like thin places either. If she travelled this way, we can, too. It may be that her protections will aid us, as well."

"As you say, Lifter."

Though she had her doubts, Jack led the way through the tunnel.

PAINTSLINGER

Drips sounded somewhere off the metal walkway. Drips that had a pattern. The numbers meant something. And as Jack listened to them, counting, knowledge came that the drips meant something. They made promises, and called to Jack.

"Ignore the drips," Jack said. The others nodded.

A smell came from under the walkway. Cakey, or yeasty, and the rust began to rain from strut and bolt.

"Faster," Jack said. Their walk became a jog.

Ahead, a wall of mist filled the tunnel. Jack used a brush to take some of the paint away and dim the light.

They stepped in.

"It's not wet," Shen Fang said.

"Cover your face," Jack said. "Try not to breathe it." She lowered her goggles and lifted her bandanna over her mouth and nose.

A hum rose within the mist. The hum that came before the chimes.

"Say," Shen Fang said.

"Run!" Jack shouted.

CHAPTER NINETEEN

Jack ran.

Something came out of the mist, and Jack used a brush on it. It's arm and wing severed and it shrieked. Another creature came, and Rosahu shoved it back from the walkway. A third, and Shen Fang met its reach with forearm and bent wrist. As it came forward, she stepped, sliding paw over the floor, in a circle. Reality dimpled in front of her, and the creature blasted away, falling off the walkway.

Some might call these things nightmares. They'd be right to say so.

Jack ran until a crumbled wall shone in the light ahead. A gap barely large enough to crawl through showed toward the bottom of the flaking cement. Jack crawled, hurrying, and waited for Shen Fang and Rosahu.

Beyond the wall, she stood in a dead bardo world with its own version of the same decayed tunnel. Rust and stalactites covered rails. In Jack's light, a black stain stood out on the crusted floor beneath them. It might have been dried blood or the tar of something crossing gap barriers, but its spatter glistened freshly. Ash drifted as flakes in the tunnel, and the light didn't seem to shine as far.

"Keep moving," Jack said, sounding too loud in the corrupted tunnel. She ran when she could, ducking under slick pipes or sparking cables. All the while, the path slanted down. More things came, all thankfully a size that fit within the tunnel.

Jack stopped at a junction, the walkway meeting a wall and turning left and right.

"Which way?" Rosahu asked.

Standing there, Jack paused. It felt like the fog had entered her mind.

Was it different here? The flame was a problem, somehow, yes. She should dim the flame, because something watched from the shadows, something that wanted her to come into those shadows and palaver.

It seemed to know her.

"Jack?" Rosahu asked.

"Say, we should move. I think something's noticed you! It can change your thoughts, you know."

"Yes," Jack said, hearing her words distantly. She realised she had lowered the flame almost to her waist.

"Two paths, paintslinger." Shen Fang said. "They smell the same to me. Can you choose?"

Focus, Jack.

Jack held the light to the right (where the shadows waited for her), the path continued in its typical decay, maybe even less than here. Safety. Jack turned and stepped into the left pathway, illuminating the space. A cable swung. Further, the walkway ended in a jagged shear of ripped metal. On the other side of the gap, the metal grate floor hung over a chasm by crumpled rails, its stalactites and rust flaked and broken.

"Here, left," Jack said. "Though I'll need help to jump." She spoke from far away, ignoring the shadows and their increasing draw on her mind.

Rosahu nodded and jumped across, then Shen Fang, and they helped Jack.

Across the gap, Jack felt her mind clearing, like fresh air from opening a window in a stale room.

"Something saw me and recognised me as a paintslinger," Jack said.

"Good thing we are leaving!" Shen Fang said.

Jack nodded and resumed walking. Better not to think about this place having a target or a grudge.

At the end of the long corridor, Jack stepped into an opening. It seemed to be the bottom of an abandoned mine shaft. Ropes hung in the centre of the boxy shaft, and around the outer walls, a small wooden staircase zig-zagged upward. Jack climbed the steps until they came to a sewer line, long and dry, and with a hole large enough that a gift demon would have been able to enter.

Jack walked first. All along the way, on wood or metal, with mist or ash around them, recent destruction marked their path. Sewer lines met a service tunnel, which led to a collapsed cellar.

Cement blocks crumbled into the path ahead with splintered wood coming down. In the middle of the rubble, a red brick wall, undamaged, looked too clean.

Shen Fang pointed. "Through there. It's not so thin. Life brews on the other side of the brick. Rain and cold."

Jack used a brush and took paint from her glove, splashed a daub of paint on the rubble. She considered, then released her flame to hang in reality here. Hopefully it could burn until Wolfgang and Kozak followed, but if not, there was the daub of paint. Her arm ached as she lowered it, looking forward to unlimited paint again.

Jack squeezed past the fallen timbre frame, stepped over cement blocks, and pressed against the red brick. It held. So Jack came back out.

"Rosahu, if you please?"

PAINTSLINGER

She moved past the rubble and pushed against the brick wall. Bricks cracked, crumbled, and sent mortar dust out as the wall slanted away then fell with a dull crash.

Jack eased herself through again, past Rosahu, and stood in the dim room. In addition to the brick wall crumbled into the space, paper crates stood in stacks, what people used to call 'cardboard.'

Jack opened the nearest paper crate. Inside, Jack saw smaller boxes and reams of paper. She held one of the smaller boxes up to the paint light hanging behind her. In an old, human tongue, the boxes alphabet symbols said, *BIC*.

Jack raised her goggles and pulled the bandanna down around her neck. Light shone from the top of the stairs along the far wall. Ancient, spark light shone from things they called bulbs.

Bulbs, old alphabets, and cardboard boxes.

The gift demon had gone to the past.

CHAPTER TWENTY

"This is the past," Jack said. "Before the canine uplift. Before generation ships."

They nodded.

"Which is to say," Jack said, "the humans here aren't going to know what to make of you both."

Shen Fang raised a hood. Better, but not great.

"Auntie, you should stay out of the light, even with your hood up."

"As you say, young paintslinger!"

Rosahu still resembled a naked, eyebrow-less bald human that might change physique at any moment.

Jack pulled off the duster and wrapped it around Rosahu. Rosahu shifted between fem and man and back to fem as she shrunk to Jack's size. But with the duster on, she could pass for human. In the low light, maybe?

At that moment, the power went out and darkness filled the cellar. Not the malevolent black of the dead bardo world, at least. Just the absence of light.

"Follow," Rosahu said.

"Yeah, follow me," Jack said.

"No. Avatar eyes," she said, pointing to her face. "You follow."

Right. Jack had no nanodrink for enhanced sight now, either. Rosahu's better vision would have to lead the way.

PAINTSLINGER

The stairs led up to a pawnbroker's shop. Old devices of all sizes, from watches and musical instruments to furniture and spark-screens, littered the space with little paper tags on them. Prices. If Jack remembered rightly, people sold their possessions to this place when times were hard, hoping to buy them back when labour tasks yielded more currency. And as deadlines passed, their hopes ended up here on the shop floor for others to peruse and touch.

A low place that thrived on the sold dreams of others. Jack understood the thin place in the cellar, now. Dreams eroded here, and in other worlds likewise. Dead dreams fed desperation, and desperation violence. Not all low places went thin, but some did, including this one.

The door hung open. Freezing rain spattered the floor at the threshold.

The street lights outside died.

"We're close," Jack said.

She stepped into the dark of a winter morning street in the rain.

A human fem youngling sat in some kind of cart or buggy on the pavement, twisted around in her seat trying to open a panel at the back. Her legs were too small to hold her weight. Mayhap the buggy was her aid.

"Trouble?" Jack asked in English. She checked Shen Fang and Rosahu quickly. In darkness of rain and predawn light, they seemed normal enough. To Jack's eyes, anyway.

"It wasn't supposed to rain," she said. "The battery's never died."

Yes. But the gift demon had passed this way, hadn't she?

Rosahu elbowed Jack.

"My companion knows something of spark-boxes. Would you like her to have a look?"

Shen Fang turned away, her back to the girl and the conversation. The girl noticed Shen Fang for the first time, her wet fur at hands and feet showing. Not good.

Jack started to give some excuse, but the girl spoke first.

"Hi, nice gloves," she said. "And boots."

"Thank you," Shen Fang said without turning around.

"No problem. And yeah you can help, but please be careful. We won't be able to afford a replacement."

Rosahu held the duster closed around herself with one hand and opened the hatch. She motioned for Jack to come over.

"It's ... d-dead," Rosahu said in Common. She opened a panel on her own shielded palm. "I can charge."

Too low for the girl to see, Rosahu revealed another panel on her forearm, and she pressed the two panels to the positive and negative leads on the spark-box. She nodded to Jack.

"Try your spark now," Jack said.

The girl turned a key and tried the forward control. It moved with a hum.

"Thank you so much," the girl said. Then, perhaps realising she spoke with strangers in the darkness, she added: "I should go."

"Good. Fare you well, youngling. Be wary of the road ahead."

She turned the buggy around and steered it up the hill behind them.

"You understand their language, Auntie?" Jack said.

"I picked it up somewhere," she said. "An old monk has time for such things!"

Jack nodded. It really was cold, and the rain soaked her clothes, now. She stepped off the pavement onto the empty road, and her ankle twisted.

PAINTSLINGER

Pain was not suffering.

"This way," Jack said, and limped along the road.

A few large buggy carts passed them in both directions with flaring spark lights on their front throwing beams in the dark rain, and the engines left an odour of carbon dioxide from their old combustion engines. These weren't for the physically disabled, like the girl's small spark buggy.

Jack's boot heel caught in a metal gutter, and she stumbled. She hit her shoulder on a light post. The last time she'd caught the gift demon, she'd spent weeks in an infirmary. And if she let herself believe that this time would be different, was that so bad?

Pain was not suffering.

Shen Fang and Rosahu likewise tripped, had clothes snag on bare landscaping trees along the pavement, and eventually a light post actually came free and fell into a shop front.

An alarm sounded from the shop.

"Hurry," Jack said.

HIGH STREET, a sign on a building said.

Jack turned onto the high street.

A few people walked by with their mobile spark screens out. They tried to shield the screens from the rain with their hands or under old rain-blockers called umbrellas. In these ancient times, people had to hold spark devices in their hands to use them, and each mobile seemed to be having problems because they all seemed frustrated, tapping hard or saying, 'Hello?' over and over again to no one nearby. Some tried to record the broken light pole, aiming their rectangles at the crumpled metal, glass, and showers of sparks.

In front of one ornate facade under a lip of an overhang, some synthetic material lay in a human-shape. A couple of broken rain-blocker umbrellas lay beside the shape and a smell of urine came from the spot.

Shen Fang moved over. The shape coughed a fluidic rattle. The breathing sounded pneumonic. Shen Fang touched the sleeping bag. Light flashed for a single moment, and the cough stopped.

Ahead, a giant shape moved through the rain at a section of the high street, past bollards where the large combustion engine buggies weren't allowed to drive. Fifteen metres tall, like seven of Jack standing atop one another with some room to spare, the cloaked demon trod.

Jack stepped, and pain shot through her thigh with a meaty snap. White hot curses of all creation shot through Jack's mind and heart. She bit them back. Well, most of them. The gift demon had broken her femur.

Jack reached for Rosahu, but her leg buckled, too, and they both stumbled. Grinding noises came from her legs, she winced, and stood, pulling Jack upright.

Another pole for a spark-light fell into a facade. Some of the humans began pointing their mobile devices at the pole resting in the crushed brick and exposed interior.

Yes, think about the pole and the spark screens rather than the hot agony throbbing through her leg. Pain was not suffering. But it was an effective distraction. She needed to keep moving. The gift demon had chosen this battle ground for a purpose.

Jack wouldn't last much longer at this rate, but they had to move now. Would the demon's wake hide the battle? For the sake of the humans here, Jack hoped so. Actually, there was a way to find out.

"Auntie, please lower your hood." Jack asked.

Shen Fang paused, then complied. The humans didn't notice. They stared at their devices, oblivious to the demon or Shen Fang. Good.

Jack released Rosahu and extended her hand. The canvas

PAINTSLINGER

shard glittered in the rain and spark lights, and began to hover. Jack opened the canvas, thinking of pain and suffering, and losing some of the relationship between those.

Focus. The shard unfolded and followed her limping steps. Jack painted a splint with a couple strokes of with titanium white. She tested it with a step, then a second. It would hold, but she was still too slow.

Or so she thought. The demon was slower. Leisurely. Enjoying its wake. If one of the humans came closer to noticing the demon, they might suffer a heart attack or stroke. Hopefully, they'd stay looking at their rectangles.

Jack walked between the bollards onto the cobbled area, where no combustion engines were allowed.

A bench collapsed as they walked by, pelting their clothes and skin with shards of metal. When Jack had caught the gift demon before, it had hidden in the future. There hadn't been so much structure around them, then. The pain still seared her memory, though: the price of the gifts.

"Hail, liar," Jack said.

The gift demon stopped.

It turned, and Jack saw the familiar raven-shaped mask covering the top half of its giant face. The bottom half grinned a skeletal grin. Its arms were held to its chest like a wounded creature protecting itself, and the hands hung limp with long bony fingers. Witch fingers, though this demon was no witch. The nails were long for when the demon desired the taste of flesh, and the tattered black robe covered the rest of the demon's body, which shifted under the folds in ways that suggested other things lived there.

"Haaaaaaiiil, paaaaintslinger." the voice rumbled low, and pleasure dripped in Jack's pain. It mocked her, toyed with her, and Jack fought down the desire to destroy the liar where she stood.

But she couldn't. Not until this curse, or whatever it might be, was lifted.

Jack had cornered the gift demon that first time at great cost and earned her prize. But the paints had not been endless. The lie must be rectified. Jack had earned her gift twice now.

Tyres on parked buggies popped up the street. A roof gave way next to them.

Jack tried to step into cat stance, weight on her back leg and front toe touching the ground. It would have to do. She drew back and threw paint out with the canvas, and sparks flew from the brush against reality as scaffolding appeared above the collapsed roof.

The ground sank in mud, and the shop fronts shifted with sparks and burst pipes.

Jack painted them back. The canvas rumbled against her paint, but it flew where she wanted it.

"Stop," the gift demon said, drawing out its speech as before, this time sounding like a child begging for her playthings. She pointed, gesturing, commanding. Jack followed the gesture. A fox stepped into the light beside the road where she'd pointed.

"End these games. You lied to me," Jack said.

The grinning head cocked sideways in a birdlike twitch.

With the other hand, the demon raised a palm and flicked her fingers and on command, combustion engines nearby revved. Behind Jack, another engine sounded.

"They'll see me," the demon said.

Lightning struck a landscaping tree on the cobble not far away. It exploded and ozone filled the air. Fire sputtering on the remains of the tree in the freezing rain.

Jack replaced the tree.

"I'm using the last of my paint, now. Even with an Eldritch

tear, my supplies diminish. Why did you lie? Do you know what it means to lie to a paintslinger knight?"

The demon waved, and the fox darted. The engines ahead of Jack beyond the demon grew louder and lights showed from a careening vehicle. Behind Jack, similar noises. The wood barrier between the bollards crashed. The motor buggies were going to collide right where Jack stood.

Jack imagined the wheels turned. If she changed the direction, they wouldn't collide at all, much less here. So she painted, sending paint to one vehicle in front of her, and the other behind, back and forth, faster. Faster still. The canvas allowed this but Jack hadn't trusted herself to use it, thusly. She was moving more slowly through time. But time acted like a spring. She'd then spring forward, dangerously fast. Those near her were affected, including the demon. She hoped Shen Fang and Rosahu were not caught in this, but there was no time to check.

"I'll escape when you stop. No gift for you," the demon said.

"I suppose you will," Jack said. "But the Sixteen Court finds its quarry."

"Jackson. You forget. You tell the truth through lies, but chaos does not. Chaos tells the truth through pain."

The demon's grin grew, if that was possible.

"We tell the truth in different languages, you and I. When death visits, or injury, people see themselves. They see life. We work together you and I. Always you and I, Jackson."

All true. But if the gift demon hadn't lied, what did that mean? And regardless, would Jack let these innocents suffer in its wake because of her chase? No. Jack put the last strokes on and withdrew the crystalline brush. She'd changed their tyre directions. The two vehicles would miss each other and be able to stop.

"This, all of this, failing paint and spells, is dragon magic. Huangdi stops your paint. Not me."

Pain was not suffering.

But sometimes, when truth hit harder than broken bones, maybe it could be.

Jack tested this truth in her mind as the gift demon turn away. Huangdi wanted magic to end. All magic, including Jack's paints. The dragon in the man mask did not want to end just her own creation and destruction, but *all* such beauty. She desired an end to samsara enough to remove the choice from others.

Had Jack known this truth all along?

In the fog of pain and betrayal, Jack hesitated. The crystal brush of the canvas vanished. Time sped up and exploded past her. In that moment, she saw there were three vehicles, not two. One more ahead of her that she hadn't seen or heard.

Too quickly, the beams of light grew and filled her whole vision. Fire, heat, and tumbling, scraping across the pavement in a rolling torrent. When she stopped, she registered several things.

Firstly, voices. Someone dragged her.

"Say, let me help you, singer!" Shen Fang said.

Blue lights flashed. Nearby, strangers spoke.

"Three drivers," one said. "What are the odds of three drivers with vehicle faults at the same time?"

"It could have been a lot worse," another said. "Lucky no one died. Minor injuries, but I'll bet these cars will all be write-offs. The builder's truck was full of tools."

"At least Sir whats-his-name will be covered."

"We should get some statements."

At that, Jack tried to move, tried to get up, but nausea flooded her with each attempt.

PAINTSLINGER

"Rest," Rosahu said.

Jack tried again, but all she could manage was feeling the top of her head. As the world spun away from her and blackness flooded into her vision, she realised: her goggles were gone.

CHAPTER TWENTY-ONE

Wylan had lost the gift demon. Stupid spider had delayed her long enough. But that didn't matter now.

Wylan's trophies were displayed throughout one of her temples. She liked living where things were worshipped. One day that'd be her as the deity.

The canvas was not displayed, though. It was hidden in a safe place.

"Stay outside," she told Asami.

"Or?" Asami asked.

"More than one way, old buddy! It's an expression. Want to know what it means?"

"No," Asami said.

"Good call. Really good. Go to one of the halls and take a seat. Take a load off. Whatever. But don't follow."

Asami nodded and walked off as proudly as ... well ... a cat.

Good enough. Once Wylan had the canvas, and with her gift from the Eldritch, it was finally time. With the dragon magic turning everything to stone, she had to act now.

Wylan would kill the dragon in the man mask. Then with her own kingdom, she'd become a paintslinger knight.

–•–

Jack woke to voices.

"The army's here."

"How? We have protections."

"They are failing."

Jack found herself laid in an infirmary. Beyond the silk curtains around her, she saw cut marble floors and solid pillars with brick walls like that of a castle beyond.

Shen Fang's home world?

A doctor came from the med-class of the canines came into her silk cubicle, likely with generations of treating patients in her family. "You're awake. Good. We kept you under while we operated, but the rest of your sleep has been exhaustion. Tell me, how much do you sleep at night?"

Jack sat up. Bones mended and pain handled. Good. She had important places to go.

Where was that again?

"Wolfgang. Kozak," Jack said. "Did they follow? Are Shen Fang and Rosahu here?"

"Yes, Shen Fang said you'd ask about them first. All accounted for, and most of them will recover fully."

Jack stood. Her medical gown wasn't the warmest thing around, and the marble floor was cool under her bare feet. But her legs supported her again. "Take me."

The emotions on the doctor's canine face were plain. "If you walk, your internal splints might not align the bones properly. The nanites could heal the bones misaligned. You need—"

"Rest, I hear you. Can you take me?"

"One moment."

The doctor stepped out, and an orderly returned with a wheeled chair. The orderly helped Jack from bed to chair and hung the bag of clear fluid from a rod rising from the back of the chair.

Smells of antiseptic, bleach, and body fluid filled the ornate halls. So many people here of all species. So many turns. The infirmary must be massive. Soon the smells of functional food added to the chemical smells, food made in large batches from simple mixes. Hospital food.

The orderly wheeled Jack into the dining hall. Hundreds of people ate and talked, but visible beyond their heads were Wolfgang and Kozak.

"Over there, if you please," Jack said. The orderly took her wheeled chair over to an alcove where her friends gathered.

"Nice gown," Kozak said.

Kozak's gown could warrant comment, but it was hard to think with all the noise and chatter around them. Of course, Wolfgang's armour never came off, it was self-made and more biological than cultural, but she wasn't without wounds. One of her two forelimbs ended in a short stump wrapped in bandages.

Hail, Jackson. Her symbols had a shake to them.

"Hail, Wolfgang. There must be somewhere quieter," Jack said.

Rosahu shook her head. She didn't seem to like this din either. She managed to escape the hospital services, and she still wore Jack's duster. She moved to take it off.

"No," Jack said. "You hold onto it. I'm not allowed to walk, much less wear clothes." Clothes were the least of Jack's worries. She remembered everything now, and seeing Wolfgang and Kozak so wounded, she wanted to apologise. But there weren't words for some things. 'I'm sorry you lost your arm' didn't quite pass muster. Kozak's wounds must have been hidden under the gown, but given the nature of the spark world, it could have been very bad indeed. An organ disappearing inside of her? Worse?

Shen Fang came and knelt beside Jack's wheeled chair.

PAINTSLINGER

She whispered, "It's okay, young paintslinger. Pain is not always suffering, and suffering is not always pain. Don't suffer for your friends' pain."

To the group, Shen Fang said, "I'm not supposed to tell you about the evacuation, but an old monk does what she wants! You'll all be moved to another facility off-world. Rosahu, you're obviously free to go as you please."

"What about the world hub?" Jack asked.

Shen Fang patted Jack's shoulder. Itching pain twinged inside her arm on that side. "We will find a way, don't you worry. The canvas is safe, and you are released from your task."

Was she now. And what would a paintslinger do with no paint?

But paint really wasn't the issue at this point, was it? Huangdi. All the crimes Jack had pinned on Wylan had come from Huangdi. Sure, Wylan had played her part, but the goodvines and how many other cultures cast in stone ...

No, Jack would find a way to paint. Now she had an obligation.

"I'll have to ask for that back, Auntie," Jack said. "Wolfgang, you are released of your oath. You have paid your debts to me in full and then some."

"Oh hell," Kozak said. "You have that look. That squinting into the sunlight pissed off look you get before you do something big and crazy."

"Uma Kozak, fare you well, and I thank you for your aid and skill with the Eldritch and with Haven. I might ask you for a nanodrink or two before we part ways."

Shen Fang said, "I'm sorry, young one. The canvas may still serve some function to us without your aid."

Jack pressed herself out of the chair. How could legs and arms itch on the inside? Still, she stood.

"Shen Fang, the Sixteen Court made those canvases, a court outside of time and space built to create and to protect creations. They belong to the Court. We may allow others to hold them, but the time may come when we require them. I require my canvas, Lifter. You may reclaim it when my task is done."

Shen Fang looked hard at Jack. Then she beamed. "I suppose it could be misplaced in transit for a short time."

You will not be alone, Wolfgang said. *Though I will ask Uma Kozak for prosthesis if she is amenable.*

"About time someone asked," Kozak said. "You all keep using the limbs you've got without thinking of what you could do with a sentient prosthetic. It changes your life, believe me. Jack sit down, you're shaking. And don't look at me like I'm an ass. Some asses are wonderful people."

Jack slumped back into the wheeled chair. Then she remembered what Shen Fang said earlier. Why were they evacuating patients?

"So," Jack said, "the patients here are being moved from the hospital. Why?"

"For safer facilities," Shen Fang said. "Why else?"

"Huangdi," Jack said. "She is coming here."

"No," Shen Fan said, "But the dragon in the man mask has sent the stone army. They are in orbit preparing to invade. They bring the magic that turns us all to stone."

"I think we've weakened Huangdi by our actions, but the soldiers will still be able to fight, and they will attack cities, not just military targets," Jack said. "Auntie, are there warriors here to fight in the meantime?"

"Oh, there are all kinds of monks here. They'll manage. But we agreed that you would only face the bard?"

Yes. That was all they'd agreed. But now Jack knew that Huangdi had changed, had chosen to change.

PAINTSLINGER

"I see," Shen Fang said. "I'm sorry."

"As am I, Auntie."

"Not to be contrary," Shen Fang said, "but how do you plan to succeed? You are healing. I'm a bit tired for an old monk! Wolfgang's lost her sword limb, and how much paint is there left?"

"I used much of it with the gift demon," Jack said.

"So no way to travel either," Kozak said, "not if you mean to use the paint when we arrive. Huangdi isn't slow of mind. You won't be able to approach by ship or by door. The felines don't help strangers travel either, and the goodvines are frozen in stone."

Jack nodded. Kozak wasn't wrong.

Rosahu saw it first. "Thin places."

"If I wanted a death sentence I would have stayed home," Kozak said. "Jack, tell her. Jack?"

Paintslinger knights had done this before. Four of them. They had tamed the thin places surrounding the old-world hub. If they could tame it, Jack could traverse it.

"It's much further than the path we took to the gift demon," Shen Fan said. "That journey bore the fortune of chaos."

It was interesting that the Lifter didn't argue. And why would she? This was what she'd wanted, after all. She'd wanted the Sixteen Court to serve its old function.

"I leave tomorrow," Jack said. "Can you have the canvas to me by then?"

"But—" Kozak said.

"I was hoping I could ask for some augmentation from an expert," Jack said.

"Flattery is unnecessary with someone as immodest as me," Kozak said. "But yeah. I'll do it. I can give you a nanodrink that will speed up the nanites, too. And yes, Wolfgang, you too. I assume you're on this fool's errand as well?"

While my oath seems to have been fulfilled, I am not ready to retire to the brush. The sword needs more practice, especially given my new circumstance.

"And you, singer?" Jack said. "You owe no debt. If anything, I owe you."

Rosahu considered then spoke. "Dark magic. The dragon takes choice."

"Huangdi makes slaves like your glamour demon did to the avatars," Jack said. "I suppose that wouldn't sit well with you."

"No," Rosahu said.

"You are brave, singer."

"Or simple. Still, w ... w-we create."

"That we do. But you should all know what we're likely to face. I've never opposed Huangdi as dragon. Dragons sing. They make. Huangdi always loved creating. She also loved tricks and traps."

And there is the stone army.

"Exactly," Jack said. "So imagine our lies to the Eldritch. We faced one enemy there, Wylan Ronde. Where we're going, the land itself is an enemy. Huangdi wanted to escape samsara, to stop creating and destroying. But she likely did that by creating in preparation, or by arranging others to create or destroy."

"Five," Rosahu said.

"You say true, singer. Five, navigating the thin places, then standing against a dragon, her traps, her songs, and her army."

"Eight," Kozak said. She waved her three arms. "My sentient limbs? Rude."

Nine if you count the forelimb you will make for me, Uma Kozak.

"Beg pardon," Jack said. "Kozak, will you make for us today so we may rest prepared tonight?"

"I already made the prosthesis for Wolfgang and the

exoskeleton for you," Kozak said. "You were asleep, and I was bored."

Jack nodded. She might be annoyed with Kozak for doing so without asking, but right now she was merely thankful. Good friends, here with her. Maybe her court was gone, but she still counted herself lucky to have companions again.

"I suggest we meet before first light," Shen Fang said. "The thin places are thinner in the witching hours." She beamed as though she'd made a light-hearted comment.

"Agreed," Jack said.

I agree.

"Sure," Kozak said.

Rosahu nodded.

Everyone shambled to feet or rose and began to move away.

Jack tried to wheel herself, failed to remove whatever brakes the orderly had put on, then sat for a moment. Could she call the orderly back?

"We all need help from time to time," Shen Fang said. "I'll wheel you."

So she did. And when Jack reached her cot in the infirmary, she was asleep the moment she laid down, even before Shen Fang left the room.

—•—

The morning came too soon and Jack felt her not inconsiderable age as she located clothes and possessions. The infirmary was already awake and abuzz, as folks prepared to evacuate. Dressing proved doable if difficult.

They met in the infirmary lobby in the twilight hours. Jack had wheeled herself using the ramps, zigzagging instead of walking straight down the steps, and so she was the last to arrive.

From there, Shen Fang wheeled her through the corridors to a room with some kind of lock. It opened as Shen Fang approached. "The medical supplies are manufactured nearby and brought to each level to be distributed. I've asked for some space to be set aside here in one such room."

Inside, Kozak's armour lay on a makeshift table. Wolfgang's sheathed blade and a new prosthetic forelimb, thinner than the width of her other forelimb, and a Jack-sized exoskeleton. It looked like synthetic metal splints that could extend or retract with her motions. Each joint was complex.

They suited up and something occurred to Jack about her new exoskeleton. "Is this one of your thinking creations?"

Kozak stepped into leg armour and answered, "Come on. I know you don't trust that stuff. I make what people need and what they're comfortable with."

Jack stood under its weight. It felt like standing and walking normally did. Her insides itched, but not the way they had when she had stood the day before. "How?"

"It's listening very, very closely to the electricity moving through your body. When your brain sends an electrical command, your limbs pick it up. Now so does that."

Wolfgang tried out her new limb. She rose to full height and used the prosthesis to strap on her blade, then tried sheathing and unsheathing.

This is astounding, Uma Kozak. The words came from the new limb. No more shake, although her characters had an unrefined shape to them.

"Use it as much as you can," Kozak said. "It starts with no muscle memory, so it relies on learning as you go. And in a pinch, try to let it do its own thing the way you used to. It's not going to react the way you would have. It will have its own ideas. Think of it like working with a teammate. Give it some freedom from time to time."

Rosahu cleared her throat and gestured for Kozak's attention. "Fuel?"

"How is it powered?" Kozak said.

Rosahu nodded.

"Lots of ways. It can recover calories from the host, or if it has more power than the host, it can actually give the body calories. It's not a parasite."

Jack moved and stretched. Good enough. Maybe one day she'd try a sentient version.

Rosahu gestured to Jack's brush-holster. "Armour," she said, clearing her throat. "And I keep this on outside?" Rosahu indicated the duster as she took it off.

Jack hadn't given something like that away since the days of the court. It felt good. Another kind of creation, giving.

"Yes. You keep it. And armour makes sense. We won't have time in the thin places, and we need to be protected to face Huangdi." Jack had planned on it, just not so soon. "Agreed?" Jack asked the others.

Nods and agreement.

"I get a mask, too," Kozak said. "Nice to see how the other side lives. Just don't put anything in the way of my sentient armour."

So Jack went from one to another. Iron white and cobalt black, masks that became faces, eight eyes, mandibles and nose holes and mouths. The voices that came from the mask were a mix of Jack and the wearer. Lastly, ornamental horns rose from limbs like frozen ebony fire, but never in a place that would hinder motion, duster, or prosthesis.

Finished, Jack took in her work, and let herself feel a moment of calm with her friends.

Then she said, "Auntie, will you lead us through thin places?"

"It would be wise to stay close!" Shen Fang said in a canine version of Jack's intonations.

"Where are the thin places?" Kozak asked.

"Why, all around us! That's why we chose this planet. Follow me to the nearest, a travel terminal that went dark."

They did.

CHAPTER TWENTY-TWO

Malevolent life grew in dark and dank corners. Prisons and war camps, cults and lying religious gatherings, in worlds who prized money and wealth over feeding the hungry and in alleys where blood spilled for material gain; in such low places, where the tortured dwelt and desires gave birth to suffering, the walls between the worlds became thin.

A malice arose in one such place. On a canine planet, this entity became aware and pressed the skin of reality until it tore. Not by consciousness or choice, but by the need to consume. As it consumed, understanding blossomed. Desires became realized and known.

Suffering made real.

Others came. Knowledge spread among such as these. An enemy was near. An enemy that opposed such malevolence.

She thickened.

She built.

She ordered and refuted and rebuked chaos.

The enemy came, yes.

But the entity was not alone. The larger things, ancient devourers who had seen galaxies birthed and consumed, were drawn here to this low place. They were cold and malignant in their perpetuity, taking joy from devouring.

In this thin place on the canine planet, where the gap

crossers amassed like vultures, the cosmic destroyers took an interest.

The defiler of thin places, the destroyer of destroyers, entered the space between.

The enemy came.

And this time, they would devour her.

–•–

Jack followed Shen Fang through empty lots into what looked like an aeroport or station.

Inside, Jack ran her hand along the top of a padded bench, and dust came away onto her paint armour. The sun rose outside and skylights let a kind of perpetual twilight gather in the huge terminal. Some kind of haze filled the space as though it was more humid inside than out. The haze had a tinge of green to it. Something wasn't quite right about it.

"We ride an underground train," Shen Fang said. "And the train always fails in the tunnel. It crosses the first boundary."

Jack nodded.

Down some grooved motorised stairs that weren't running, another terminal with spark displays showed departures.

PLTFRM1   DELAYED
PLTFRM2   DELAYED
PLTFRM3   DELAYED
PLTFRM4   DELAYED
PLTFRM5   DELAYED

"Why not cut the power to this place?" Kozak asked, gesturing with her prosthetic third arm.

Shen Fang paused to look at the displays. "We did."

PAINTSLINGER

"Oh. Oh right. See, this is why I don't come to the thin places," Kozak said.

The board display flashed static, some scene of violence, then changed.

PLTFRM1   DELAYED
PLTFRM2   DELAYED
PLTFRM3   WELCOME! BOARDING NOW!
*   ENJOY YOUR JOURNEY!*
PLTFRM4   DELAYED
PLTFRM5   DELAYED

"Demon?" Rosahu asked.

"Maybe," Jack said. "Some thin places live, though. It might be the place itself."

The motorised stairs started, and music played from elsewhere in the terminal. Dust swirled in eddies ahead of their steps. Good that they were wearing the masks and armour. No telling what harm might be in the air around them.

The platform lights were lit below, but so dark as to hurt the eyes.

"Kozak?" Jack asked.

"Already on it. Here."

Kozak handed around the nanodrinks to allow vision in this darkness. Odd, drinking through the mask. It allowed ingestion just as it did breathing, but everything lost a little flavour on the way.

No train stood at the platform. Vision grew to show a swept floor, but with deep black spatter stains in the crevasses and corners.

The tannoy squealed, then spoke, *"Next train arriving in four minutes! Four must be your lucky number, travellers!"*

Shen Fang looked around. Again, if she was worried, Jack was worried.

"Have you been here before?" Jack asked.

"I have," Shen Fang said.

"It's always like this, right?" Kozak asked.

Shen Fang didn't answer.

The tannoy again. *"Here the train comes! We've been waiting for you, Jack."*

Light shone in the tunnel. A shape ran in front of the light and brakes squealed. A popping noise, and the train rolled onto the platform with lights flickering in the cabins.

Something glistened on the front of the train as it slid to a stop a little too far from the platform edge.

The door parted in the middle, opened too fast, then slammed shut again. Open and shut several times, shaking dust from the fixture and handles inside, then stood open.

Right.

Rosahu moved to go first.

"Hold," Jack said.

"Being b ... b-brave?" Rosahu asked.

Jack shook her head, held a finger to her lips, and then pointed to her armour. Because what kind of painter would she be if a door could crush their magical armour? Well. Depending on the door she supposed. This being a magical door, maybe she should think this through.

Or ... just get on with it before endangering others.

Jack stepped onto the train. The engine revved, but the door didn't budge. Which was enough of a relief that Jack was glad of the mask. At first Jack thought they might be cramped, but the train seemed larger than she'd expected. It was the standing kind, meant for quick boarding and exiting, with bench seats along both sides. Everyone boarded and stood except Wolfgang.

A couple things happened very quickly, then.

Wolfgang drew herself into the door, and it moved razor-fast.

Wolfgang moved faster.

She turned with prosthetic limb and caught half the door. It squawked and squelched and tried to slam, but she held it.

"Let it go," Jack said.

Wolfgang looked at Jack and spoke in a voice half-Jack's. "I shall. But first I mean for this place to understand the nature of our visit." She bristled in a way only she could, rising and taut, then ripped the door out of the track. It sounded like a scream.

"I think it gets it," Kozak said.

"We shall see," Wolfgang said through the mask.

The train started smoothly after that.

The lights flickered out.

Kozak's armour glowed blue through joints. "Save the paint, Jack. I've got this."

In the light of Kozak's spark-glow, the door showed whole. It was back.

The speaker cracked. *"Enjoy your stay! Enjoy your stay! Enjoy your stay!"* Louder and louder, over and over again. The train sped up, faster and faster so that the acceleration and rocking made it hard to stand.

The whole carriage jolted, and Jack found herself slammed into the bench seat.

"Brace!" Jack shouted. The train was going to derail at this speed.

Jack felt herself come off the floor, then all was pain.

In the pain, Jack knew she tumbled around inside a literal train wreck. She felt herself collide with the others and with the poles and seats. The sound of metal-on-metal screamed through everything. Sparks and flames flashed. Every time

Jack thought it was over, another jolt or shift sent her into someone else in the strobing light.

Eventually, Jack realised the train had stopped, and that the spinning was in her equilibrium. She rose to her knees, pain shooting through all her limbs, and threw up. The mask allowed that, too. Sadly, it didn't help the taste coming out.

"We're outside?" Rosahu asked.

Focus, Jack.

"The first barrier," Shen Fang said. "Paintslinger?"

Black regolith under Jack's fingers felt sharp against her grip. Light from the train wreck's flames flickered against the obsidian rubble. They must have been thrown free of the train in the wreck? Good they had paint armour, then.

Jack rose, stumbled, and finished rising. Good. She could do this. She just had to get her bearings.

An alien landscape surrounded them, pocked and scarred, like the surface of a recently dead planet, at least as far as light allowed them to see. Giant slug trails, three metres wide, criss-crossed a torn terrain and some kind of scaled foliage. Fire flickered from the train crash. The glow from Kozak's armour still shone, but there was no sun, moon, or stars.

This was the space between worlds. Inside the thin place. Only this time, no gift demon concealed them in its wake.

Jack checked on her friends. Rosahu changed from man to fem, the armour adjusting as she morphed. They circled together and stood a few metres from the twisted metal of the train carriage and the mouth of the tunnel.

"Okay," Jack said. Because more complex sentences weren't coming.

"Enjoy your stay!" continued on a loop in the ripped train until the wreckage behind them jerked back into a tunnel as though pulled by some giant monster. Which, all things considered, it might have been.

"You think it 'understands the nature of our visit'?" Kozak asked, shaking head, body, then stretching one leg at a time.

"Not yet, obviously," Wolfgang said. "It will."

"We need to move," Jack said. "Auntie?"

Shen Fang dusted herself off. "This way. It would seem this place has something personal against you, Jack. Why might that be?"

"Art critic," Jack said, and spat.

"Jack. You made a joke!" Kozak said, and clapped her two-side prosthetics.

"Don't tell anyone," Jack said.

"This way," Shen Fang said. "It smells more wrong this way."

Kozak gestured down. "Uh, problem."

Between the obsidian rubble, red light bloomed. Above, sparks began to swirl and drift toward them like fireflies.

"Quickly!" Shen Fang said.

She disappeared and reappeared further ahead. "Come!"

Jack ran.

She had never seen fire gap crossers, but as they followed under the surface and as the sparks blew behind to follow, flickers of doubt came into Jack's mind. Had she actually gotten up, or was she lying in the train wreckage, still unconscious? What if she only dreamt she was running, and this was a ploy to keep her motionless and prone as monsters killed her in her sleep?

"Hurry!" Shen Fang said. She blipped out of existence, appearing next to Kozak, then disappeared again, jumping Kozak forward in space. She did the same to Rosahu, and then Wolfgang. Jack noted the futility of these heroics, and for some reason, thought of the walkway in the other thin place, and the shadows that called her there.

Jack slowed to a stop. Maybe the sparks weren't actually

bad. Mayhap they circled her to help her wake. She needed to stop dreaming, stop running and playing into this farce because the dream was an illusion and she was stuck in it.

"Jack, run!" Rosahu said.

"Don't touch her," Shen Fang said. "The fire lies to her now."

But, of course, she hadn't said that because this was a dream. The train wreck and then this dream.

Rosahu nodded, bent her knees and pulled her fists to her waist. A tonal chant came from her mask, the song cutting across the doubts in Jack's mind. It felt like fresh air in her thoughts, pushing out clouds of sulphur.

"This is real?" Jack said.

"Good!" Shen Fang said. "Continue, singer!"

"This is real," Jack said. Fireflies caught up and touched Jack's armour, and pain radiated from the touch points.

"This is going to feel a little weird!" Shen Fang said. She appeared next to Jack, and then Jack felt herself ripped out of reality.

Pain faded, and Jack appeared in another place, another dark landscape, only this one had a moon. No, two moons. Black liquid splashed off her to the swampy mud as though she'd just risen from some tar pool and sent a spatter of it around her.

"Don't move," Shen Fang said.

She vanished and reappeared with Rosahu. Black ichor flew from Shen Fang as she stumbled into this plane of existence. Kozak and Wolfgang next.

"What the hell was that?" Kozak asked.

"We don't speak of it. I wasn't supposed to do that," Shen Fang said. "It leaves wounds"

"It aims for my mind," Jack said. "The thin places are targeting me. I thought I was dreaming."

PAINTSLINGER

"Hold fast, paintslinger." Shen Fang said. "You have many enemies here. And, I think they remember the four paintslingers from our past."

Yes, four came before and never returned. Four minutes until the train. A bad number. The number of death.

The masks all showed worried faces.

"Rosahu, can you help?" Kozak asked. "Or does running mess up the magic song stuff?"

"Can't," Rosahu said.

"Auntie, please lead us further," Jack said.

"As you say, paintslinger. The mountain ahead," she said. "It sleeps. Don't wake it."

The steps on this plane of reality felt long. It felt like Jack walked for kilometres in mud under the two moons. Maybe she did.

They took a meal at some point. Jack relied on her companions to feed her. Her hands kept trying to arrange the rations into good shapes. Her mind existed in a kind of twilight rather than act on impulses because her impulses were being tricked, manipulated and tugged.

Did vision go? It might have. And sound, intermittently. It made Jack's mind hurt.

Something rose at one point, something too dark, something treelike only writhing, and she painted it away. Her friends thanked her for saving them, but that was a blur now because thought was pain and doubt.

They climbed into a dead tree to escape that world.

The next existence had no gravity. They were in a mine or a huge quarry with only the cool light of Kozak's spark glow creating a pocket of vision. A sound like backwards echoes rippled through the space.

Shen Fang and Rosahu tried to help them anchor to a rock wall, but they seemed to be tiring.

"Hail, lifter. Hail, singer," Jack said. Her mouth was dry. She wanted to take off the mask, but a part of her understood that the armour had probably mitigated the attack on her. And they were flagging.

"You're back?" Kozak asked.

Jack see-sawed her hand. Not quite.

The backward echo came again.

No.

"This is bad," Jack said. "Auntie, how do we get out of here?"

"I need to remove my mask," she said. "Can't smell it any more."

Ah. So that was why Jack was better. Maybe some of the darkness of this place had refocused on Shen Fang.

"The things that live here are a different kind of gap crosser," Jack said. "They see us in time. So if they can see us—"

"They have seen us," Kozak finished.

"A lyst," Wolfgang said. "Pan is against us today."

Echoes almost had words in them, now. Their words? Their planning?

"To me," Jack said.

Not that there was anything Jack could do against the lyst, but she would try.

Had the four ended, thusly? Trying?

In zero gravity, they climbed their way across the slick walls in the pocket of light from Kozak's armour. It felt like being deep underwater.

Jack gestured to Rosahu. "Can you help Shen Fang?"

The canine fumbled with her mask, and Rosahu tried to keep the lifter's hands from hurting herself.

What had she said back on the Eldritch plane? *You touch reality when you paint. There are other ways to touch reality, young one. I helped you along when you needed it.*

As Wolfgang and Kozak joined her on the wall, Jack drew her brush. Not to paint, but because she could feel reality with it. The texture of the real pressed ever so lightly against her bristles. Bodhisattvas above, it was so thin here, she could barely feel it.

Thin.

She pressed, and the brush dimpled reality.

Jack put her brush away and felt with her armoured hand.

"Take hold of me," Jack said.

Rosahu held Shen Fang with one hand and touched Jack with her other. Wolfgang and Kozak gripped each other's hands, and Kozak put a prosthetic on Jack's other shoulder.

"Do you know what you're doing?" Kozak asked.

"This once, Kozak, no I don't. Not at all." Though she did have a theory. Shen Fang had brought them along this route intentionally. It was possible that the neighbouring reality led to Huangdi.

"I liked you better lying," Kozak said.

"Fair enough," Jack said. She felt with her hand. Nothing. She moved it where the brush had pressed and, yes. A slight impression. Reality. Like when she'd pulled it away from the glamour demon, only this time she would rip it, tear it and go through like Shen Fang had.

Jack pushed.

Reality ripped a little, a black slit under her touch, and Jack fought the urge to recoil. It felt like a wound, barely torn. "Hold on," she said, and pressed harder.

And fell, sucked out, the skin of reality scraping her as she passed. It wasn't like this with Shen Fang. This was more like the seeking stones, only no pearls. No light. No shifting form.

An eye. Oh gods, an eye.

Jack twisted, felt for reality but it wasn't there.

She drew her brush and slashed.

Reality tore, a wide gash, pulsing, but the gash was better than the eye. Jack braced, jostled, and stopped as something pressed at her from all side.

Underground. Buried?

Jack tried to twist, to make sure the rip was closed. She couldn't move. She had taken them to a grave.

Yet a part of her relaxed at that. Not because she'd given up, but because the grave was a natural place. Perhaps the most natural after birth. It was a thicker place than where they'd been. And it was a place they'd all go eventually.

She tried to think of what to say to the others, if they were buried with her. To laud them and praise their bravery. To hope she'd meet them in the next life.

But before she could, a hand plunged into the earth and gripped Jack's armour.

No, not a hand. A paw.

Jack took it, and she rose.

CHAPTER TWENTY-THREE

Back at the Court of the Man Emperor under the red giant sun, Wylan walked past a burnt gate into the ruins of the palace. Pillars and stone walls ended short, and no ceiling stood. Wood smouldered and flickered, sending plumes of smoke into the air, making her eyes water.

Statues from the menagerie, blackened and flame-blasted, moved and scurried past, carrying swords and bows.

A canine statue passed in front of her. Wylan grabbed it by the shoulder. "You. Where's my palanquin? My pillows?"

It looked at her for a long moment.

"Oh whatever. Just take me to the Man Emperor."

It led the way through the fallen palace to an airfield where a courtyard used to be. Hundreds of zeppelins were arrayed and tethered. Stone soldiers in queues led to each, loading munitions.

And on the edge of the airfield, a man stood watching with arms crossed behind his back. He wore singed linens, sooty at the sleeve and the cuff of both legs.

"Hello, Bard."

No twisted horns behind. The doll stood freely. The doll was human. He turned and faced Wylan and held up a hand in a gesture for her to stop.

"You seem surprised."

Wylan felt for her lute, her hands finding only her ripped and filthy kimono. Stupid spider. Could she reach her ward brush in the back of her kimono before one of these soldiers turned on her?

The man smiled. "Yes, despite your failures, I stand mortal. Fortunate for me, I have other servants."

Other servants ... that might succeed him?

"My Emperor, how may I serve you now?" As in: can I kill you?

He shook his head. "A death here would not be permanent. We would find ourselves in the same cycle, creators prolonging us all. Our only escape is destroying the creators. I will destroy Sixteen Court."

He'd gone mad.

"The court fell," Wylan said.

"Did it now? Even for the rogues that remain? Those that can traverse time?"

He meant to travel in time and destroy the Sixteen Court. No, prevent the court entirely.

It would fracture reality, billions of minds going mad.

Wylan breathed. Focus on the speed of the ward brush.

"My Emperor is wise," she lied.

She reached.

A stone grip clamped on her wrist and held her arm behind her back. The blackened canine statue that had guided her. Wylan twisted, and it gripped her other arm.

"My emperor?"

"No more games, Bard. You are released of your oaths. But I will give you a gift. You will know how we travel." He smiled.

Wylan strained against the grip, and the stone squeezed. There had to be a way out of this.

"Murders, tortures, malices: they mirror sometimes, don't they? Where prisoners are buried alive to weep and suffocate, a malice can grow and rip," he said. He turned to a passing statue carrying supplies. "Ready my zeppelin."

He looked back to Wylan and gestured. The canine statue turned Wylan and pulled her, half- dragging until she walked.

"Thank you for your service, Bard. Your last service."

-•-

Jack ached with the force of the pull on her arm. Above, someone dug, exposing more of her arm, then her shoulder. Her lungs tried to pump, stinging as she held them still.

The paw released her, and then a familiar hand pulled her hard. Rosahu's armoured grip hefted, and Jack came free of the rubble.

"Thank you," Jack said. "Are the others—"

"Safe, yes," Rosahu said. She gestured to Kozak, who dusted herself off and Shen Fang, who pulled, helping to free Wolfgang. Then she waved her hand over the scenery. "Where are we?"

Indeed. Tiered gravestones, taller than a person and spaced at four metre intervals, rose around them in dying light. Jack stood in a mountainside graveyard, surrounded by bare pine trunks, the wood black and dead.

"A graveyard doesn't go thin," Jack said. And yet here they were.

A biped feline stood to the left, digging into another grave.

"You helped us, stranger?" Jack asked.

"Asami," she said, digging still.

"I'm Jack, and I say thank you."

A blur moved, and Jack felt herself pushed aside. She hit a gravestone and toppled it, then steadied herself.

Wolfgang now blocked her view of the feline, heaving.

"Brushmaster?" Jack said.

"She was with Wylan, Jack. She is an enemy." Wolfgang held up her armoured prosthesis.

Jack stepped around Wolfgang between them. "Do you defend yourself, Asami?"

Asami didn't answer. She stood, facing away, toward the fog outside the pine trunks. A glow grew, there, brighter, and brighter still. Lightning, blue and hot, flashed, covering everything in for a split second, until—

Jack saw a vision. It reminded her of Shen Fang's gifted sight from the stone banyan forest, only this was an intrusion on her mind, cutting across thought.

Jack saw a man in pale linens with sooty sleeves and legs, standing on the deck of a zeppelin high in the sky. Despite whatever distance the vision crossed, Jack knew him. Huangdi. He had looked so, before, in another life. When he spoke, the words touched her mind intimately and uninvited.

"Jackson," Huangdi said, "did you think I wouldn't feel your magic armour and wards? Your spark and spell? I've felt you across universes, and you come to my home and palace, brazen as always. Did you think you could stand against a peace that has turned entire planets to stone? No more. Our cycle ends today."

He waved his arm over a sky full of zeppelins like his, stone soldiers filling the decks.

"My servants on land and in the air do not come for you today. We will go through you, to the source of this cycle. This is my gift to you, and to us all."

White hot throbbing grew behind Jack's eyes. She shut them but still saw the light. It throbbed larger, and distantly, Jack felt gravel under her knees as she fell.

And then it stopped.

CHAPTER TWENTY-FOUR

Jack blinked, trying to focus as the splitting ache in her head dimmed. She knelt in the graveyard. A wind gusted through, lessened, and whipped again.

Footsteps crunched beyond the gravestones.

Jack stood, willing the canvas to expand around her. The fractal gem shard grew to a thin crystal frame around her. She needed to question and puzzle how Huangdi had escaped dragon form. But everything had happened too quickly.

A stone solder ran out of the fog.

Crystal brushes formed in her hands, and she dipped and threw the paint, removing the golem's legs. It fell to the ground, silent.

After a brief gust coming from the same direction, Jack felt the ground vibrate. Footsteps. More than could be counted. An army.

"Did you see the vision?" Kozak asked. "How did Huangdi even do that?"

"Dragon magic," Shen Fang said. "Odd, since Huangdi seems to be mortal, now, yes? Still, we aren't becoming stone."

"I saw it," Jack said. Though it made no sense to her. Still, she had an idea. "Rosahu, Wolfgang, on guard. Auntie, please help me dig. Kozak, we need to know what's coming. Can you send a golem?"

"It's called LIDAR, and yeah, I've got it," Kozak said, and detached a piece of her spark armour in the shape of a thin rod. She drove it into the gravel, and it telescoped upward.

Wolfgang, for the first time, hesitated. She looked a long time at Jack before finally gesturing an affirmative, and moving. So Jack finally found the limits of the oath?

"Thank you," Asami said, drawing Jack's attention back.

No time to reflect. Jack dug quickly, beside Asami and Shen Fang, with her hands until she came to wood. A charred coffin lid showed shallow in the earth.

"Here," Kozak said. "I printed you a tool like you should have asked."

She tossed a metal bar with a curve at the end to Shen Fang, who caught it and pried at the edge of the coffin lid. The wood cracked and splintered.

Wylan Ronde, the lazy one, wriggled. She was bound and gagged and filthy. She blinked, breathing heavily around the rope and cloth in her mouth. She strained against the rope tied to ringlets drilled into the coffin bottom. Her eyes widened at Jack.

Jack reached in and untied Wylan from the coffin, leaving her wrists bound.

When she was out, trying to pull the bonds from her wrists and cursing, Jack spoke. "Firstly, free this servant from whatever oath you hold over her."

"Nice armour, gang. Really swell. And her? Why, she's a dear and true friend, isn't that right ... you?" Wylan said.

"She told me I would die if she died," Asami said to Jack. "This is why I dug here. I searched for her."

"Say, that ward is forbidden!" Shen Fang said.

Wylan rolled her eyes. "It's already undone. My warding brush is gone."

The sound of stone crashing against tree came up to the

graveyard, and a shout from Rosahu, rhythmic. Flame flared in the fog, and more sounds, this time metal meeting rock. Wolfgang's blade was drawn, it seemed. They had met the first of the army.

"Secondly," Jack said, "you'll tell us how Huangdi changed, and then I'll imprison you here for your crimes until we are finished with our task."

Wylan rubbed her temples. "I saw the vision, too, Jack. Pretty neat, right? I wish I knew how he became mortal. But the problem is, our man emperor is all crazy now. Huangdi plans to stop the Sixteen Court from ever forming."

Another flash of fire beyond the gravestones, this time catching the bare trunk and lighting it. The army grew closer.

"That's impossible," Jack said. "Huangdi doesn't paint."

"Painting isn't the only way to fly, sweetheart," Wylan said. "Thus, my early burial. He desecrated these graves and made a thin place here, which is pretty impressive if you've got an army large enough to keep you comfy along the way, am I right? There's a gigantic mausoleum up the mountainside wide enough to send an army through, zeppelins and all. He'll travel by thin place to the past. As soon as his army is supplied and ready."

"Ronde is right," Kozak said. She gestured with her prosthetic, and a holographic view of the landscape appeared in bright orange monochrome. "This is us. Behind these trees up slope, look. It's the mausoleum," she said as the lines and dots redrew themselves to zoom out. "And here is what's downslope."

The perspective moved, back down past the miniature graveyard, past tree trunks on the downward slope, to a river, then open marshland. To left of the wetland, a dense tangle of forest, much thicker, though also apparently bare. To the right, a shoreline and ocean. And ahead, the ruins of a castle.

"And this is who's coming," Kozak said. As she spoke, zeppelin balloons materialised in orange, towing passenger decks, each filled with soldiers. At the rear of them, closest to the castle, a giant zeppelin, quadruple the size of the others, flew with banners waving from the decks. On the marshland below, rows of golems marched in ranks. The view swung back to the graveyard, where miniature versions of Wolfgang and Rosahu fought two dozen soldiers.

"These must be scouts or runners," Kozak said. "There are too many for us to fight, Jack."

"Say," Shen Fang said. "You saw him. You know where he is. That large zeppelin. You've seen it."

Yes, Jack had. She could paint herself next to the man emperor, Huangdi, a mortal at last. But how did he become mortal in the first place? And on succeeding, why hadn't he just stopped, and chosen a mortal end? He wanted to cease, not travel across time to the secret location of the court. It didn't add up. This was not the Huangdi she knew.

Maybe that was the problem. Jack expected Huangdi to stay as she remembered, as she'd loved and hated throughout time and battle without count.

Huangdi had changed.

But what of this army? What if the soldiers persisted? As golems, they should have already died when Huangdi became mortal, crumbling with aeons of age.

"Kozak, can you stop the army from getting into the mausoleum?" Jack asked. "I will handle Huangdi, but they can't be allowed to leave this world."

The spark view in orange zoomed back up to the gaping carved entrance into the mountain, pillars on both sides. Kozak touched the view, and graphic diagrams circled the bases of the pillars.

"If these were destroyed, I might be able to collapse the

opening," Kozak said. "That would just delay things, though, right?"

The ground shook, and the trees downslope burst into the graveyard, toppling and crashing into headstone towers. Cordite smells hung in the air. Wolfgang.

Jack started toward the sound, but Wolfgang emerged, limping from the fog and the fallen trees. She barely held her sword, her jade brush gripped by her other forelimb. Rosahu supported her on one side.

Wolfgang came to Jack, stepped too close to Wylan, almost crushing her against a headstone. "We have only a moment," she said coldly in mixed voices. "More come."

"Why do you delay, paintslinger?" Shen Fang asked. "We must go to Huangdi."

Because of the army. There was a way Jack could destroy this whole world, the entire army. And was she avoiding seeing Huangdi in person? Maybe.

"Kozak," Jack said, "try to collapse the mausoleum as you suggest."

"Got it," she said. "I'll do all the hard work, as usual."

"Wait," Asami stepped forward. "There are prisoners in the palace, held with song. I won't leave them."

"Boring," Wylan said.

"I'll g ... g-go," Rosahu said.

"How will you go? Through the army?" Kozak asked.

"I can take you," Asami said. "By the joins at the corners."

"Jack," Kozak said. "More soldiers are coming. They're at the base of the mountain. We've got a minute, max. Are we doing this?"

Could Jack go with Asami and Rosahu? Paint there?

No, that would leave Kozak and Wolfgang trying to stop the army, and besides, Huangdi could sense Jack. He would know she had travelled and attack there rather than here.

"What about me?" Wylan said. "I'd rather not go crazy in a broken reality. You don't really mean to leave me tied up, do you?"

Wolfgang raised her blade to Wylan's neck.

"Hold, Wolfgang," Jack said. "Wylan, stay with Kozak, and stay out of the way."

"You've got to be kidding," Kozak said.

"Sorry," Jack said. "Auntie, will you guard me while I paint?"

"As you say, paintslinger."

A whistling sound came, and an arrow clattered to Jack's left. The army was here.

Jack raised the crystalline brush.

CHAPTER TWENTY-FIVE

Jack didn't start the portal to Huangdi. She turned to the sky, stepped into cat stance, weight on her back foot and toe touching in front, and dipped the crystal brush of the canvas into her paint.

She imagined what she'd seen outside reality.

A destroyer. It was the only solution. Kill Huangdi. Stop this army from leaving the planet.

She threw the paint. It exploded away from her in a line to the sky, cutting the atmosphere with a smell of ozone and destroying reality between her and the stroke of paint. For a split second, before the clouds rushed into the vacuum created by the farpaint stroke, a queasy grey patch sat between the star and this planet, visible, and uncomfortable to see.

"Paintslinger!" Shen Fang shouted. "A destroyer? No! This is not the way!"

A tree fell nearby, resting on grave stones. A stone golem rushed in, running on the fallen trunk, bow drawn. Others were close behind. A dozen or more.

The group exploded into movement. Wolfgang rushed to intercept a squad of soldiers with her jade brush. Rosahu grew and blocked a pair of golems. Everyone reacted in their own way, fighting.

Jack turned from her farpaint. The destroyer could wait.

She dipped into her bandolier and slashed her brush at one a golem that rushed past Wolfgang. The soldier split at the middle and crumpled.

"Take us to Huangdi!" Shen Fang shouted, her gravelly bark louder than Jack had ever heard her. "Take us to the emperor!"

"Kozak, move," Jack said. "Wolfgang?"

"I will push them back," Wolfgang said, mid-ward. The golem crumbled at her feet. Another replaced it. Then another. She was in a rhythm now, holding the line.

"As you say, blademaster," Jack said, turning to the others and letting Wolfgang work.

"Come back in one piece, singer," Jack called after Rosahu, who hurried away with Asami.

"I w ... w-will," she said, moving away up the slope between graves and bare wood.

Jack watched her friends leave, gave herself a single moment to appreciate Kozak's augmented paint and spark armour, Rosahu, armoured yet wearing Jack's old duster, Wolfgang, grunting with a voice, part Jack, as she rushed between the graves to fight countless enemies. Even Shen Fang, stepping into a short stance with arms extended in front of her, ready to redirect any attack.

"No more arrows getting through, Auntie," Jack said, resuming her farpaint. A few more strokes. She opened the way.

"You must not do this," Shen Fang said.

But Shen Fang was wrong. This is exactly what Jack must do. The planet was a seed of malice. If not stopped here and now, it would spread across the multiverse.

Jack shifted stance, her weight centred between front and back leg, knees bent, and raised her off hand. A brush appeared there, too.

PAINTSLINGER

The picture in her mind, again: the terror at the cosmic malice. Jack sent paint rocketing into the sky.

Vaguely, Jack was aware of movement around her. Shen Fang attacked soldiers, disappearing with them in her grip, reappearing elsewhere, and throwing them with the momentum.

Jack rocked her weight between front and back, throwing paint with both hands, feeling the buck of the canvas as she pressed the brushes against reality with each stroke. Sweat poured under her armour. Left arm, right arm, repeating, and the itch in her bones returned as exhaustion pressed against all of Jack's body.

A patch of skull hung there. Though the sky blocked the view, as the contrails of relativistic speeds burned the atmosphere, Jack felt the destroyer, searching. It was coming through to this plane, and it would destroy this world.

Two things happened, then. The ground shook, and a deep concussive bass sound moved through Jack. A sound that built, growing louder. The earth shook, more and more, as the vibrations built.

"Problem!" Kozak shouted. "Run!" She slid into view between trees and kept going, heading downslope toward where Wolfgang fought.

"It didn't work?" Jack asked, collapsing the brushes.

"It did work! That's the problem!" Kozak said. "Landslide!"

Pieces of rock and pebble shook loose. Upslope, at the edge of the fog, the trunks tilted toward Jack.

She ran.

"Auntie, warn Wolfgang," Jack said.

Shen Fang vanished.

Beyond the gravestones, Jack rushed into the foggy forest. The ground still shook, but she kept her footing. An arrow sailed into view and hit the armour of Jack's shoulder, and another hit the canvas frame itself. Jack was glad neither arrow had struck her joints in the armour that allowed movement. All the while, the vibrations coming up into Jack's legs increased. Boulders tumbled behind her. She needed to reach the flat ground.

A golem emerged from the fog. Jack dodged under its reach, turned, slashed colour and removed its legs. A trunk fell, crushing the remainder of the golem.

Jack glanced back. The rolling wave of dust and rock billowed huge in the forest, pushing the trunks down ahead of it. Dust filled the air, surrounding Jack.

She wasn't going to make it. Jack took in the colour of the earth, and braced her back foot, digging the heel into the scree. She willed the brushes into her hands, and they appeared. Jack dipped two-handed, into bandolier cartridges at the front of her armour. She slashed paint upward from the ground. Buff titanium, raw umber, and a rock overhang stood in front of her, parting the landslide. Not enough to stop the tonnes of rocks falling down, but the small shelter would buy her time.

Jack turned, slid a short way, and resumed her run down the slope.

A tree trunk fell to her left, and she ducked instinctively despite it already having landed. Did her legs feel less vibration? Was she getting ahead of the landslide?

The fog was thinner here, and Jack made out shapes of Wolfgang, Shen Fang, and Kozak ahead, running down the slope ahead of her. Soldiers blocked their way, ready to die in the landslide to stop Jack and her friends from reaching the flat ground. Wolfgang cut through a soldier with her blade and shoved another aside before sending a ward with a flash, cutting a path through the line of golems.

Beyond them, light played over running water.

PAINTSLINGER

Jack reached the last rows of trees and chanced a look backward. Rocky dust now filled the forest. The sounds of sliding gravel still came to her between the trunks, but the earth no longer shook.

Jack emerged, stepping on the level pebbles in the shallows of the river, which was twenty metres wide. She stopped between Wolfgang and Kozak.

Standing in the ankle-deep water and trying to catch her breath, Jack understood the size of the army for the first time. Kozak's miniature spark display in the graveyard hadn't conveyed it like a one-eighty view. Above, hundreds, maybe thousands of zeppelins flew. They darkened the evening light over the marshes like a storm cloud.

And in the marshes, above the waist-high grass, endless rows of golems marched.

Some had reached the river, and they waded through low water toward Jack and her friends.

"You see?" Shen Fang said.

An arrow sailed in a high arch toward the canine. Wolfgang jumped in front of her, slashing the arrow in flight and landing hard.

Jack did see.

If Jack finished painting the destroyer, it would come too late to save her friends and would take days to destroy this planet, devouring life and hope, and driving everyone on it insane while drinking in their pain by the hour.

But if she stopped Huangdi directly, there was a chance the army would stop, too. Not a guarantee, but yes, a chance.

"Be ready to come with me," Jack said.

"What?" Kozak and Wolfgang said at the same time.

"Through the portal," Jack said. She stepped into the ready position, then a high sumo stance that would allow her to twist quickly at the waist. Two brushes appeared in her hands, the crystals cool to her armoured grip, and Jack prepared to paint the person she never wanted to render again.

She pictured Huangdi as he'd stood in his zeppelin, the way the skin stretched over cheekbones, his linen clothes with burn marks and sooty black stains, and the smoky air whipping through the open deck. Brushes dipped in cartridges, colour came out thickly, and Jack touched the bristles to reality. The canvas hummed, and reality pressed back. Liquid sparks flew from each application, as Jack plied paint to the texture of the real.

She remembered how he'd chosen to look in a time long past. Jack could have painted him with a nanodrink, but she would not need *CLEAN REMEMBRANCE*, now that Huangdi had forced the vision of his new form upon her. His hubris and his gloating would aid her. Some of the details she'd forgot returned. The way he tilted his head—part curiosity and part condescension. The open-palm gestures he gave that suggested both command and patience.

She imagined him now in such a position, arm out over the battlefield, ordering the army and knowing, at his core, that he deserved this victory. She painted him, thusly, three-dimensional, and then she painted the zeppelin deck as she'd seen it.

It wasn't alive, yet, though. The bubble in reality, three metres tall, was static.

Distantly, Jack was aware that her friends moved around her, likely fighting the soldiers as they came out of the water, but her mind was here, trying to bring him to life. It wasn't working. Why?

Jack put more paint on, at first thinking of the lemon yellow and cadmium orange for the warm tones of the wood deck, but soon working by rote, unthinking about which colours came from her bandoliers, twisting at her hips and pushing the layers of paint onto reality. It should have worked by now.

She stood straight up and walked around him until she looked at his face.

This was why. She'd made his face surprised to see her, and in her hubris, she'd believed he would be. But no. He wouldn't be surprised. He'd known it would come to this. Huangdi had forced Jack's hand.

On his face, she painted a knowing smile.

Smoke and cool air from that altitude came through the bubble.

"Now!" Jack called. And taking a deep breath, she jumped through.

CHAPTER TWENTY-SIX

Jack faced Huangdi, took in the sight of him, as her friends came through the portal and stood beside her.

"Watch the portal," Jack said. "Don't let anything through."

"Nothing will come through," he said.

"Huangdi, I—" Jack said. She could do this. She could end this reign, all the injustice, everything, here and now.

"Jackson," he said, the wind of the heights whipping his thin, linen shirt and trousers against his skin. "You finally got your canvas back."

"I tried to stay away," Jack said.

"You always do," Huangdi said. He stepped to the edge of the zeppelin and opened the waist-high gate. "Is the secret kept?" He paused there, holding the rail of the deck and lifting his foot out over the empty air as though he'd step out and fall. Only then, looking at him standing so dangerously close to a kilometre drop, did Jack see the deck texture itself below his feet. The part she hadn't painted had scratches, deep scars in the wood, like scale and horn and claw had rested here.

"Enough, paintslinger," Shen Fang interrupted. "End this."

"Wait," Jack said. It couldn't be. The claw marks ended exactly at the part she had painted, which she'd made whole. She'd changed the zeppelin, depicting it.

"You see it now," Huangdi said. "You see how you've helped me."

"What is he talking about?" Kozak said. "Why isn't he fighting?"

"You never intended to end the court," Jack said. "You did it to bring me? But why? I prolong you. You want to die."

But Huangdi the dragon couldn't die. And with all the magic of the multiverse, always prolonging the immortal, the change would likely never be complete. As long as Jack had continued, and Wolfgang with her wards, and even Wylan in her novice laziness, the dragon would never be able to become the mortal, to become the mask.

There was another way, though. If someone painted Huangdi *as* a man ...

The vision was a trap. A lie. Huangdi the dragon had been here, hidden by a sleight of hand or light.

Jack had made her mortal.

Huangdi slowly released the rail, arms out as if welcoming an embrace, and leaned back.

"Wait," Jack said. Maybe because of the justice he deserved and could now meet, or maybe because he could command the army to stop. Jack couldn't say. In any case, she didn't get time to consider it.

Movement from the corner of her eye, and Jack should have known. Shen Fang bent knee, and then vanished.

Jack looked to Huangdi, just as Shen Fang appeared in front of him. All the momentum of her vanishing and reappearing went into Huangdi as she pushed, palms out, onto his chest.

Huangdi closed his eyes, hurling away from the canine with incredible speed and force, and then fell.

Jack went to the edge and watched Huangdi die.

—•—

"It wasn't your place," Jack said, facing Shen Fang.

"It was no one's place. There is no court, paintslinger. You are a rogue, accountable to no one. Look in the sky. The half malice grows. It will come through, and devour this planet. Would your court allow you such power? To destroy worlds?"

"Art is power. This is exactly what we do. Create when we can. Destroy when we must."

"We had plans for this place. It touched many worlds. You broke the highest laws there are."

"For now," Jack said.

"For now!" Shen Fang agreed. "Say, I guess we need a Sixteen Court, then?"

Layers of truth, as always.

"Did you know that I would make Huangdi mortal?" Jack asked.

Shen Fang nodded. "I did. The dragon magic still held. It was the only way."

"Look," Wolfgang said.

Distantly, a zeppelin crashed into its neighbour, driving both into a third. That one descended, its deck ropes snapping, swinging free. But stone soldiers didn't fall. Only eddies of dust, swirling in the quick high-altitude wind. The soldiers were gone.

To Shen Fang, Jack said, "Then we are enemies. You are an enemy of the court."

"Such as it is!" Shen Fang said. "You owe me a canvas."

"On that, Lifter, we differ."

Jack walked across the zeppelin deck and stepped through the portal onto the river bank.

—•—

PAINTSLINGER

Jack saw Rosahu and Asami were already there, a crowd of people with them on the river banks.

Thick dust lay on the pebbles and drifted as soot through the shallow river. Golems, disintegrated, had returned to dust, clay, and mud.

Jack waited for Wolfgang, Shen Fang, and Kozak to come through, then she removed the portal to the zeppelin and painted another. As she depicted the forest where she first met Shen Fang, her paint stores diminished none at all.

Jack stepped through into the light of the two moons.

EPILOGUE

The moons' light on the forest floor was natural, with no malice, and the green grass brushed calmly against Jack's ankles as she stepped into this world.

Jack removed armour and mask from her friends and Shen Fang. Asami didn't come, and Wylan, Jack realised, had vanished.

Jack painted the portal away.

"I suppose no meal for me tonight, eh?" Shen Fang said.

"No Auntie. Not for you."

"A pity. Maybe in your court one day?"

"I doubt it, Auntie."

She nodded knowingly. "Fare you well, paintslinger. Keep your secrets, and take care of that canvas."

Jack waited for her to leave, then stumbled.

"I've got you," Kozak said. She helped Jack to a tree trunk, then set up and printed a metal gazebo. After, she kindly created crutches for Jack.

Shall I assist you with tent and meal, Jack? Wolfgang said, voiceless once more without the mask.

At first Jack thought to say no. But with the crutches, a little help setting up camp wouldn't be amiss.

"Not like the old days," Jack said. "The two of us limping about."

PAINTSLINGER

No, it isn't like those old days.

The rest of the set up was silent, until Jack asked, "You're going?"

Tonight.

Jack considered arguing, or trying to convince Wolfgang, but the oath had been kept, and choices could not be unmade. Nor should they be. So she finished setting camp in silence.

The tent set and the meal prepared, Jack invited everyone into the shelter. She sat and ate with Kozak and Rosahu, though Wolfgang ate separately.

After their meal, Jack found Wolfgang outside the tent. "Thank you, brushmaster. Fare you well. The blade or the brush, now?"

The blade is for the young. I will study the brush, now. She hesitated, then said, *Thank you, paintslinger. I will see you again.*

With that, Wolfgang set off through the forest toward the town and spaceport.

"As fun as it's been, I'm catching a ship," Kozak said. "Nature isn't really my thing."

"Where to?" Jack asked.

"Once a standard decade, the most brilliant minds in the worlds gather and share ideas."

"Are you invited?" Jack asked.

"Very funny," Kozak said. "I'm the main event. If they haven't cancelled while I was away. Of course, you'd take me out of communication range. You're such a hermit."

"You aren't wrong," Jack said.

Kozak moved toward the gazebo to gather her things, then paused. "I left you something in your supplies."

"As you say, maker."

Jack watched Kozak gather her possessions until Rosahu

stepped out of the tent. The singer started to take off the duster.

"Keep it. It suits you," Jack said. "I'd have your attention for a moment, if it pleases you."

Yet Jack saw she had no such thing. Rosahu wasn't simple or slow, she knew what Jack was thinking.

Still, Jack had to ask. "I was fortunate to work with you. If you liked, we could continue to collaborate."

Already she was shaking her head. "Much to see, paintslinger. My heart is in the stars.

I will c … c-catch a ship. With Kozak."

Jack tried to think of a way to change her mind, but words, as they so often did, failed.

Rosahu loped away, changing between male and fem under the duster as she walked. She and Kozak set off into the forest.

Jack considered staying at the empty camp, and decided against it. Instead, she gathered her supplies, mixing tent and old brushes, food enough for a couple days, and inside a pouch, she saw what Kozak had left her: two vials of nanodrink with the words *CLEAN REMEMBRANCE* etched in common on the glass. Yes. A good gift. Jack put it all into a pack and set out.

Jack walked alone.

In a clearing, not far from a peepal tree, next to a small stream, Jack unfolded the canvas. Was she going to set up a new Sixteen Court now as Shen Fang wanted? No. But there were four paintslingers lost to time that had helped build a world hub before. Jack needed to find them. The secret must be kept.

One of the crystal libraries in the space castle worlds might serve her purpose.

Unlimited paint rested on the canvas's crystalline bristles that hummed with life and power.

Jack began to paint.

THE END

ACKNOWLEDGEMENTS

Thank you to my kind readers for joining Jack on her journey.

This book would not exist without my family and dear friends. You know who you are.

The credits at the front of this book are too small to do my collaborators justice. Thank you Elizabeth, David, Jennifer, and everyone at Dark Cosmos Creative.

ABOUT THE AUTHOR

Jeremy K. Hardin has contributed to 26 films, television shows, and games in his career as a digital artist, and enjoys exploring worlds in his writing.

www.jeremykhardin.com